PENGUIN

Aisling's
Diary

Aisling's Diary

AISLING FITZSIMONS

PENGUIN
IRELAND

PENGUIN IRELAND

Published by the Penguin Group
Penguin Ireland, 25 St Stephen's Green, Dublin 2, Ireland
(a division of Penguin Books Ltd)
Penguin Books Ltd, 80 Strand, London WC2R ORL, England
Penguin Group (USA) Inc., 375 Hudson Street, New York, New York 10014, USA
Penguin Group (Australia), 250 Camberwell Road,
Camberwell, Victoria 3124, Australia (a division of Pearson Australia Group Pty Ltd)
Penguin Group (Canada), 90 Eglinton Avenue East, Suite 700, Toronto, Ontario, Canada M4P 2Y3
(a division of Pearson Penguin Canada Inc.)
Penguin Books India Pvt Ltd, 11 Community Centre,
Panchsheel Park, New Delhi – 110 017, India
Penguin Group (NZ), 67 Apollo Drive, Rosedale, North Shore 0632, New Zealand
(a division of Pearson New Zealand Ltd)
Penguin Books (South Africa) (Pty) Ltd, 24 Sturdee Avenue,
Rosebank, Johannesburg 2196, South Africa
Penguin Books Ltd, Registered Offices: 80 Strand, London WC2R ORL, England

www.penguin.com

First published 2008

1

Written by Helen Bagnall
Based on the TV series *Aisling's Diary*,
created by Nuno Bernardo and written by Melanie Martinez/Róise Goan
Copyright © CR Entertainment 2008

The moral right of the author has been asserted

All rights reserved
Without limiting the rights under copyright reserved above, no part of this publication
may be reproduced, stored in or introduced into a retrieval system, or transmitted, in any
form or by any means (electronic, mechanical, photocopying, recording or otherwise), without the
prior written permission of both the copyright owner and the above publisher of this book

Set in 10.5/15pt Sabon
Typeset by Palimpsest Book Production Limited, Grangemouth, Stirlingshire
Printed in Great Britain by Clays Ltd, St Ives plc

A CIP catalogue record for this book is available from the British Library

ISBN: 978-0-141-32672-6

www.greenpenguin.co.uk

Penguin Books is committed to a sustainable future
for our business, our readers and our planet.
The book in your hands is made from paper
certified by the Forest Stewardship Council.

Contents

Last Exit From Boston	1
Somewhere Over the Atlantic	11
New Girl	20
Just Murphy	28
School Project	39
That's Magic	50
Flashmob	62
Step Up	73
Making Up	105
Dance From the Heart	130

LAST EXIT FROM BOSTON

Saturday 23 August

Seven days before moving to Dublin, Ireland. Nine days before starting at new school in Ireland . . . and counting!

4:20 p.m.

I, Aisling Louise Fitzsimons, am on the eve of a new adventure. One in which I leave everything I have ever known in my young life: Boston, Charlestown High, friends Amelia, Lauren and Colleen, Sean Nós Best Dance Academy and object of my affections, Phil Donnelly (more of him later!).

One in which the sixteen-year-old heroine (that's me) travels many miles over the ocean to Dublin, Ireland, in search of a new life. Wait a minute, what am I talking about? That sounds way too dramatic. What's really happened is my dad lost his job as a plumber and decided that it was time to move the whole family back to Ireland where he and my mum met and where I was born. OK, so the real story's not quite so Hollywood but either way I have decided to chronicle the whole affair.

So welcome to the extraordinary adventures of Aisling Fitzsimons.

Sunday 24 August

Six days before the move! One week tomorrow I start a new school.

6:45 p.m. (Day Two of Aisling's Big Adventure)

Today may not have been extraordinary but it certainly was delicious. Fajitas and Ben and Jerry's Rocky Road – two of my favourite things – although, believe me, they don't taste twice as good if you have them together. This I know. Hmm, I'm not sure recording my disastrous cooking experiments counts as an adventure. I will have to keep a proper eye out for more extraordinary things when I get to Dublin.

I went to Irish Dance class with Amelia and Colleen. Afterwards we went back to Colleen's to watch the new *Camp Rock* DVD. Did a new dance routine, which was part Irish reel, part *Step Up* 2. Either way it was SO cool, if he were ever to see it, Phil Donnelly would wish he was going out with me and forget all about Jen Brettmann. Jen or Tinker Bell (because that's the role she played in the End of Year Show). How awful would it be if Phil chose a girl called Tinker Bell rather than me? Especially when the only reason she even went for that role was because she got to wear a sparkly silver leotard. There's no way Phil would choose a girl in a silver sparkly leotard over the Regional Irish Dance Championship Finalist 2005, is there? Tinker Bell was so annoying at the after-show party, and when Phil and I were chatting and messing around she kept appearing, talking about how difficult it was to 'act' with silver wings, and asking Phil if he'd seen her 'performance'. He had to listen to be POLITE but it was really embarrassing. Hmm, another note to self: when we move to Ireland, make sure less embarrassing things happen to you. Yeah, like that's going to happen.

We had a bit of a chat about the scale of gorgeousness. Amelia doesn't think Phil Donnelly scores very highly at all and gave him a three. Colleen, however, can actually *see*, and agrees with me he's off the gorgeous scale.

Less than a week till we make the move to Ireland. Arghhh. Will they have fajitas? Will they have Ben and Jerry's Rocky Road? I just don't know.

Wednesday 27 August

This is A-MA-ZING. Finally, something worthy of my chronicles. I was coming out of the math room when Phil Donnelly's mate Woody ran up to me. He said 'Irish (Phil's nickname) wants to see you after school by the tennis courts'. I played it cool and just nodded. Amelia, however, lacked my inner composure and started shouting 'Oh My God, Aisling, Irish wants to see you after school by the tennis courts' like some kind of mad parrot. Anyway I'm getting SOOOO distracted, so then after school I went over to the tennis courts and he was waiting there with Woody and Billy. He said 'heard you're going to Ireland?' I said 'yeah, next week'. He said 'what day?', and I said 'Saturday'. He said 'that's really cool – Ireland, that is, not you going' and then SPOILER ALERT he looked really sad and said 'won't be seeing you around then', and then he said 'see you around, Fitzsimons', and then he KISSED ME ON THE CHEEK. Nothing this good has *ever* happened to me.

6:54 p.m.

What's that bumping sound? Oh yeah, it's me coming right down to earth. Have just realized that even if Phil asks me out – I am still moving to Ireland and will never ever see him again apart from on trips back. How altogether tragic is that?

Thursday 28 August

Move Saturday. New school Monday.

Not much to report of the extraordinary nature. Mainly spent the day wondering about the unfair nature of love and wrapping up knick-knacks in loads and loads of paper. Thinking I might become a minimalist in later life, purely to avoid having to wrap up hundreds of Beatrix Potter figures only to unwrap them on the other side of the Atlantic. Maybe the gods will be kind and the ship with all our stuff will end up at the bottom of the Atlantic with the *Titanic* and all the dead fish.

Got a bit carried away with a daydream that Phil never ever forgot me and dedicated his life to coming to work in Ireland to track me down. One day I was coming out of a tea shop in old Dublin town (work with me here) and there he was waiting for me on a big horse, carrying a picnic basket full of fajitas and ice cream. 'Fitzsimons,' he said, 'I've put a cup of tea for you on the stairs' – but then I realized that was in fact my mum saying that and not Phil and the whole thing was ruined.

Went to my last ever Irish Dance in Boston. The last time I'm going to get changed with all the girls. The last time I'm going to tap tap tap through to the dance room. It feels weird to think I don't know where I'm going to be for the next class, who I'll change next to, what the teacher will be like. Weird, scary and exciting all at the same time, like watching the Spiderman movies.

Friday 29 August – The Farewell Party

Am forced to hide in my room because the adults have been doing a version of partying for what seems like hours now. I think everyone we've ever met since we've been in Boston is in the house right now. I even saw my old middle-school teacher Mrs Brown (or 'Jan' as my parents insist on calling her). Even Mr Shilpa from the Health Food store was here at one point. How many times I have heard 'The Wild Rover' played tonight: 34 approx.

It was all pretty cool though, there were loads of people here I hadn't seen for ages. Mum and Dad sure do have a lot of friends in Boston. At one point I got a bit sad thinking I didn't know when I would see everyone again. But I'm sure we'll be back, we're only going a little way around the world. At one point I found my eleven-year-old brother handing out business cards with his 'details' on, although just why Rory thinks Amelia, Mrs Brown (Jan) and Mr Shilpa need his details I just don't know.

8:45 p.m.

'The Wild Rover' again? What's *wrong* with these people, is it, like, really the only tune they know? Ah yes, that would be it. Would be bearable if I couldn't hear Rory joining in – surely as my younger brother he should have been in bed *hours* ago. No wonder he looks like he does with such disregard for beauty sleep. Oh, yes, now I get it. ☹ That's why he looks like that.

Saturday 30 August – The Day of The Big Move

10:32 a.m.

So the day's finally arrived, which is great for lots of reasons but mainly because it means I won't have to watch Dad wandering around the house, packing and singing his dirgey music, or 'Bob Dylan' as he calls it, really loud, because the stereo's unplugged. You think he'd be more excited to be going home to Ireland – it *was* his idea after all. Maybe he had a little too much of the Guinness last night – there are certainly a suspicious number of cans in the recycling box. Got to go because I am in charge of BREAKABLES – KITCHEN.

11:07 a.m.

Mum thoughtfully packed Dad's stereo away in the first crate. He wasn't happy – because he wanted to 'supervise' its packing. Rory kept making this joke: What's worse than listening to your dad's music collection? Having your dad *singing* his music collection. I tried not to laugh because one of the rules of being an older sister is that your little brother is NEVER EVER funny. What was also funny was Dad shouting 'Steady on, careful' to the mover-guy who was packing his records. You honestly would have thought mover-guy was packing the crown jewels and not some old pieces of plastic made by hippy types from the way my dad reacted. Actually I think one of the mover-guys got a bit annoyed with Dad when he told them for the fourth time to put more paper round each record because I saw record-packing guy raise his eyebrows at the KNICK-KNACKS & ODDMENTS guy. I don't blame him – they're only a few records, right? What a *fuss*.

12:13 p.m.

I bet you can't guess what happened? I can't believe it! I went back into my room to find all my Irish Dance trophies are just loose in a box. I hung around the landing a little bit moodily giving the mover-guys my Aisling Hard Stare until they asked me what was wrong. I asked them if they thought my (hard won) under-14s Regional Championship Golden Batters trophy was going to make it to Dublin OK without ANY packing paper to protect it? They sheepishly told me that Mum is doing the kids' rooms. Kids? I'm *sixteen*. I raised my eyebrows at Rory but he wasn't looking so I'm not sure it really worked.

2:00 p.m.

Disaster! Where has Betsey Mouse disappeared to? I had a terrible vision that she's lying at the bottom of one of the crates under loads of *Friends* box-set DVDs. I'm not sure she'll survive that, she's at least 100 years old in toy mouse years. Although she's not a mouse – I KNOW – but as I always tell people, I couldn't say 'rabbit' when I got her and it's too late to change now.

The man who had to completely unpack every case didn't look all that relieved when we found her in the SHED MISC. crate. I actually think I saw him raise his eyebrows as well. What is this, National Raise Your Eyebrows Day? Hey, maybe the guy has a medical affliction of the eyebrows. If that were the case, wouldn't my dad feel bad for being horrible to him? Think on, Daddio. Talking of Dad, I heard mover-guy tell him that unpacking cost extra and Dad went a bit pale. Well, someone should have made sure Betsey Mouse was not in the shed, shouldn't they? She has been with me to every Irish Dance competition I've been in. Coincidence? *I don't think so.* I can't just abandon her because I've got way too old for a toy mouse . . . er, rabbit.

4:00 p.m.

Amelia came round – she'd printed off loads of pictures of all the Irish Dancing crew and put them all into a scrapbook with all the programs and everything we'd done. I felt really sad after she went, I wanted to go and lie on my bed, but I couldn't because it had been packed. Luckily, Dad had been out for donuts 'for the workers' and I felt a bit better after a raspberry-filled glazed Krispy Kreme. They will have Krispy Kreme drive-thrus in Dublin, won't they? I mean, it *is* a civilized nation.

When Amelia left, I remembered that I hid Betsey Mouse in the shed when Phil Donnelly (gulp) was coming round to do math homework last month – as I didn't want him to know I still had a cuddly toy. Decided not to mention this to the parents, they'd only start with their 'why didn't you remember any of this BEFORE the man unpacked all of the crates'. Whoops.

Maybe it's time to get rid of her? How though? I can't just cast her out into the garbage (oh sorry – I have to say 'rubbish' now), can I? Maybe I'll take her to one more competition and then burn her.

Did I just say 'burn her'? What am I *thinking*? I can't *burn* her. Anyway gotta run – we're late (as usual). Paddy Cabs (as Dad calls them) are here to take us to the airport.

It's taking us ages to actually get out of the house, everyone forgot at least one thing. And then Mum and Dad took ages to say goodbye to the house, they walked round every room. It's only a *house*. We've even got another one to go to in Dublin. Sometimes Dad seems not to remember that it was him who wanted to sell up and move back home.

We're on our way. Woop woop.

5:57 p.m. - airport lounge area

I was OK until we were all in the cab, because who knows when I'll be back again? I started to think about how much I was going to miss everyone. I had a quick look at the pictures on my phone. There's some of Amelia and me that I hadn't seen for ages. I was turning around in the cab to take one of our house and then I saw Phil was on our street. He was walking towards our old house. He must have been coming to say goodbye to me because he had what looked like a big bag with a gift in it and a balloon with a shamrock on it. He walked up to the house and knocked at the door. He looked really nervous – he kept trying to look in through the glass. I was waving like mad to get his attention but he didn't see me. He was standing there getting smaller and smaller as our cab was driving away. How much would I have liked to run down the stairs and open the door to him, but instead I was getting further and further away from him. How much does that suck?

Boarding, we're boarding. Everyone's running for the gate. Quick, betta rush. I want to get the seat away from Rory to ensure peace and harmony for the next six hours.

6:01 p.m.
At last on the plane. Got the seat two rows away from Rory. Peace and Harmony is mine.

6:45 p.m.
Peace and Harmony totally over. The man next to me is so fat his thighs are seeping out of his space and into mine. Gross.

Just eaten. Yuck. They said it was Irish hotpot but I would call it Irish horri-pot. If that's what I have to eat each day then I just might set myself up as a one-woman fajitas and Krispy Kreme import business. That way I can be sure I won't starve to death. The man next to me fell asleep and his head was bobbing FAR too close to my shoulder. I kind of put loads of pressure on his arm and steered him over to the other side where he started bobbing *on* the shoulder of this Japanese woman. Which was much better.

Rory played *Tetris* on the plane computer with the other kids. One of them in particular was almost as excitable and annoying as Rory. The two of them were just hanging out in the aisle causing a complete disturbance, so much so that the hostess couldn't even get her trolley down the aisle. You think she would have sternly told them to go back to their seats like some kind of headmistress but she just kept asking them loads of questions and laughing at their answers as if they were funny and not totally idiotic. So in the end I had to wait *ages* for my Coke, which when I got it was so tiny that even a baby flea would still be really thirsty after drinking it. I thought of asking her for another one but she wasn't laughing at anything I said so I was too scared.

SOMEWHERE OVER THE ATLANTIC

Saturday 31 August

1:54 a.m. Dublin time (8:54 p.m. Boston time)

Not only have I got a raging thirst but now the lights have all been turned down really, really low – I think the general idea is we all fall asleep. All the stewardesses are huddled at the back on little flip-up chairs eating food they brought with them. I bet they want us to go to sleep for a bit so they can all sit at the back and moan about us all. Bit of a swizz that, isn't it – we've paid good money for our tickets, so surely that deserves table service AND a bigger Coke? I bet *they* don't have to eat Irish horri-pot. I KNEW it – one of them's brought their own Wendy Hot Tex Mex chicken in a bun. My mouth is literally watering.

How annoying's that? Rory's just arrived back at his seat with four little cans of Coke. FOUR. He 'accidentally' bopped me on the head with one while getting back into his seat and then said in a really annoying voice, 'Oh did you want one of these?' I said 'no', meaning 'yes' of course, but he just did his really annoying smile and gave one to his *Tetris* pal. I couldn't even go back to my portable DVD player as the battery's gone – the in-flight entertainment has only got films I've seen before – all of them *boring* – most of them about a girl who meets a guy with a dog, from what I can see.

2:43 a.m. (only Dublin time from now on – time to adjust, Aisling)
I'm so excited about moving to Ireland. But no matter how many times I think about it, I can't get it straight in my head. At the end of last term I was at school at Charlestown High in Boston with my friends Amelia and Lauren and the Irish Dance gang, but Monday I'll be at a new school with new friends and a new dance class. What will it all be like? Will I fit in? Will they like Irish Aisling? Of course they will. Everyone likes Irish Aisling.

But will I ever get over Phil Donnelly? Who knows the answer to that one? I will have to get Amelia to check to see if he is showing signs of missing me and record any details by email. Good idea, Aisling!

I wonder what Ireland's like? I know there are no real leprechauns, but I think shamrocks and Guinness are real. I can't wait to be close to my cousins and my aunties and Granny Nora again!! Yay, Granny Nora. I can't wait to see her.

I can't really remember anything about Ireland no matter how hard I think. I remember it's really, really green, there are loads of fields and – and I remember some old men dancing with proper brushes to jump over with fiddle music in the country one time – but that might just be from *Waking Ned* and I've got a bit confused.

What I always end up thinking about is when Rory MADE ME (just in case adults ever read this) give the sitter the slip last year on St Patrick's Day and then MADE ME dance outside all the Irish centres in town for Irish revellers in the big foam green and white hats. Actually I think Rory still owes me my ten per cent. Maybe Ireland will be like St Patrick's Day in Boston every day?

I wonder if Amelia's right and I'll get an Irish boyfriend? She says all the men there are, like, totally gorgeous, and I've got to email her some pictures of all the guys in my class by the end of the month. She totally flipped when I said I was going to Ireland and said she would never, ever get a new best friend, but then she said she was really jealous because I would get a 'new' Irish boyfriend. I doubt it because no one can ever replace Phil Donnelly – I will never forget him. Us Fitzsimons are loyal that way.

3:46 a.m.
Hey – maybe I'll get a boyfriend like Gerard Butler in *PS I Love You*.

5:23 a.m.
Watched four episodes of *Father Ted* to get in the mood for Ireland, Father Dougal is *so* funny. AWFUL thought. Argghhhh. What if all the men in Ireland are like that and not like Shane from Westlife! I shall have to become a nun and help the poor. Are nuns allowed to Irish Dance? Maybe there's a special order for Irish Dancing nuns. Hmm. Make a note – must look into it. Gotta go now, the seatbelt sign has come on and the Japanese lady is trying to shrug the man off her shoulder. Ha ha. You snooze, you lose, lady.

Who knows? Have officially lost track of time
Just arriving in Ireland now. Dublin does not look like Boston from the air: I kept looking out for the Bunker Hill Monument and had to keep reminding myself that this *isn't* Boston. There were so few lights, no wonder the stewardesses turned the lights down, otherwise we'd look like Vegas itself coming in to land. As we were landing, I saw Dad look at Mum and say 'well I guess that's it – no turning back now' and then Mum smiled and touched him on the arm. They do state the obvious at times, the adult folk, don't they? OF COURSE THERE'S NO TURNING BACK. We're in a plane

hurtling towards the ground with wheels on. I guess you don't need much physics as a plumber, do you?

Middle of the Day But Feels Like the Middle of the Night

So, get this, it's the middle of the morning but although I'm in bed I obviously can't sleep because it's bright light out there. We were made to go to bed when we got here like we were little kids. More evidence that adults are stupid? Like, as if we'd be able to go to sleep. I should be looking around our new neighbourhood not staring at the poster my cousin's put up of Britney Spears in a school uniform, listening to Rory snoring.

Uncle Conor came to meet us at the airport – it took us ages to come out because our luggage has taken itself off on holiday to Timbuktu rather than Dublin. That's always where luggage goes, isn't it? Never Belgium or Canada. Hey maybe that's just airport-speak for 'we have no idea where your luggage is, but we're working on it'. By the time we actually came out Uncle Conor was looking pretty bored.

We all piled into Conor's car and they took us for a big long ride round Dublin. Mum kept saying 'Oh' really loudly every time we turned a corner. Which was then followed by a 'Look, John, that used to be the Ritzy', or 'Look, McSweeney's is now a T-Mobile store'. *So* boring. Dad didn't say much, and only muttered when Uncle Conor kept saying, 'Glad to have you back, John' and 'Listen to that engine, you can't hear a thing, German engineering that is'. Is that what Uncle Conor thinks is good conversation: German Engineering? What next: Swedish Forestry? Albanian Farming. Ye gods.

Uncle Conor and Aunty Stella took us to see our new house, which we move into tomorrow. Hooray. It had a big banner on it saying 'Welcome Home, Carol, John, Aisling and Rory'. HOME in big red capital letters. It's nice, a bit like our house in Boston but much smaller and much closer to the other houses. In fact everything about Dublin seems so much smaller than home.

Home? What do I mean *home*, this is home now. Isn't it?

As I was getting out of Conor's car, I saw a scooter at the house next door. There was a guy on it about my age but he wasn't dressed like any of the blokes at Charlestown High. He wore tight dark jeans with a studded belt that said 'He of the Dance Floor' – or something – and a bright blue polo shirt. Then. He. Lifted. His. Visor. OMG, let's just say if Irish men look like that I don't have to worry about finding that convent for dancing nuns. Ha ha.

Oh – I'm quite tired now. Byeeeeee xxo.

PS Hero of the dance floor. His belt must have read 'Hero of the Dance Floor'. Yeah, right, what do the Irish know about dance floors?

4:00 p.m.

New school tomorrow. I've decided I'm going to take this opportunity to develop the more sophisticated side of my personality. As Posh charmed the society of LA, so will

I, Aisling, charm the society of Dublin. I will ask myself what would Posh do before answering any question, never smile and always look demure.

5:00 p.m.

Have been practising Irish Dance in the mirror and can't see Posh in the outfit OR the ringlets. Ha. And it's much too hard to try to be her without a David Beckham look-alike, so I think I'll just be myself instead.

I do, however, have a little speech worked out for tomorrow. I was thinking 'Yeah, I'm Aisling, that's my name. Don't wear it out.' Like Danny from *Grease*. Or I could go all deep south, 'Why yes, it is *the* Aisling Fitzsimons, the one who has won so many competitions for Irish Dancing in her home state of Massachusetts. So very pleased to meet you.'

Maybe it will be like when Colleen started at Charlestown and we all crowded round asking her about a million questions about where she was from and what her old school was like. Hello I'm Aisling I'm from Boston in Massachusetts, yeah it is kinda cool, I guess, but I'm happy to be your friend.

6:00 p.m.

Mum has already found out about the Irish Dancing classes so I should not go too long without a practice. Yay, but guess what? I was showing my planned outfits for the week to my mum when she told me that I have to wear a uniform. Ex-squeeze me: a 'whattiform?' You should see it – it's ker-azy. It has a funny little white shirt, a really scratchy skirt and a tie and everything. Rory came in and tied the tie round his head and was running round like someone at Wimbledon – that is, of course, if any tennis players had the body of an eleven-year-old REALLY ANNOYING BOY.

6:10 p.m.

Hey guess what? I think I can make a few moderations to el uniform, which will make it, like, really cool. Amelia's gonna laugh her socks off when she sees a picture of me in it.

10:00 p.m.

Am lying in bed too excited to sleep. Uniform hanging on the back of the door with a few exclusive Aisling Fitzsimons-style alterations. How funny to think I won't be the Irish girl like I was in Boston, just an ordinary schoolgirl who's come back home to Ireland.

11:00 p.m.

How annoying is *this*? Put on my shuffle to listen to a bit of Alicia Keyes to help me sleep. To find my brother has loaded all his horrible rap music on it. I kicked him awake to ask him about it and he said, he had to in case his music didn't make it because – get this – his music is all rare stuff whereas mine is all rubbish. The *cheek*. He was still dancing to Barney when I had my first PCD single. Oh well – I'll try to find an instrumental on his iPod. He MUST have something restful.

11:10 p.m.

No joy. Am wide awake and realize that if I fail all my exams and my life is ruined because of this incident of no sleep it will be the fault of:

- Rory
- Jay-Z
- Pharrell
- Missy Elliot

In that order. You know what, Jay-Z? I've now got ninety-nine problems and a little brother IS one.

New school tomorrow. Arrrghhh.

Late O'Clock

OMG. I can't sleep. Every time I close my eyes I keep thinking of going to school tomorrow. Every time I open my eyes, there's the uniform hanging on the back of the door reminding me how I have to go to school tomorrow. I keep thinking about how I have to walk into the classroom and have everyone turn round and look at me. How will I find my way round? What if nobody speaks to me? What if nobody likes me? It will be OK, won't it?

NEW GIRL

Monday 1 September
3:55 p.m.

The horror. The horror. The horror. Have just got back from the worst day at school anyone's ever had. Am going downstairs to see if a huge number of ice-cream scoops can make it all all right (which I doubt). More later.

Later

List of bad things that happened to AISLING FITZSIMONS today. I just hope you've got enough time to read all of this.

1. Eavanne and Sorcha (more of them later, unfortunately). Yuck.
2. Dozy Miss O'Connor got my name wrong. She introduced me as Aisling Fitzpatrick and everyone laughed. She then made me do an introduction to the class about myself. Even though I had my little introductory speech ready, it felt really silly. Nobody smiled. So I just stammered through something and sat down. Nobody was really interested in who I was. It wasn't like that at Charlestown when Colleen started.
3. No one alters their uniform here. Not even a bit. They all wear them shapeless and boring with a FAT TIE. Mine was tighter, shorter with a THIN TIE. Disaster. How to Look Like the Newbie 101.

4. I got lost in the corridors and didn't know where to get any lunch. I asked Eavanne and Sorcha and they made fun of my accent. And then one of them said 'someone should tell her she's not in *The O.C.* any more', which doesn't even make sense because *The O.C.* is in California, which is at least 3,000 miles away from Boston. Even though it was obvious Eavanne was geographically wrong, Sorcha still laughed. Which shows how stupid she is.
5. Lunch. No comment.
6. There is no Irish Dance 'gang' for me to join. This I now know, because a girl called Siobhan told me. Why? I still don't know.
7. No email from Amelia, Lauren, Penny or even Colleen. Did get the standard monthly newsletter email from Charleston Phoenixes saying they won the State Regionals. Without me. Argghh again.

List of good things that happened to AISLING FITZSIMONS today.

1. This girl Siobhan was really nice to me. She also told me all about the boy next door on the scooter. Previously referred to as the man who saved me from a life as a dancing nun by being off the scale in terms of general gorgeousness. He's called Murphy. No second name. Just Murphy. Like Sylar from *Heroes*.
2. The End.

List of CATASTROPHIC information which I, AISLING FITZSIMONS, received today.

1. Murphy is going out with Eavanne.
2. Argghhhhhhhhhh.

4:35 p.m.
Just remembered that Mum is the very woman who told me fairies and Father Christmas were real. I learnt at a very young age not to rely too much on that woman's grasp of the truth. Maybe Irish Dance, Irish style will be terrible.

Rory was really making me laugh in the garden though with his new moves. Honestly, that boy met Lupe Fiasco ONCE in New York and you'd think he had actually been on tour with him for several years the way *he* talks about it. All the kids in the neighbourhood were watching him. 'Excuse me, I'm the dancer' I wanted to shout but I kept a dignified silence, like Nicola from Girls Aloud does when everyone's going on about how good-looking the girls are. But I would like to point out that *I* was the one who spent hours in Amelia's bedroom looking at YouTube break-dancing videos and copying them move by move. But I don't like to scream and shout about my talents. For example, if I had been made class captain today, like Rory, I would not have found it necessary to tell everyone, including all my family, cousins, people I've only known two days and even to announce it on my Bebo page. How gauche (new word

– think it means common, heard Aunty Stella calling some of the women on the estate gauche).

PS Eavanne and Sorcha are gauche.

6:30 p.m.

There I was patiently trying to explain all about my day to Mum and Dad over fish-fingers, when Dad gets up halfway through to take a call on his mobile. Then he actually went off to go and fix someone's immersion heater, and I'd only got halfway through number 3 on my list. Umm, hello?? Daughter's happiness important to you at all? He would never do that in Boston – he's really changed since we got to Dublin – there's, like, Boston Dad and then there's Dublin Dad and they're as different as chalk and cheese. I should perhaps start another list of all the ways he's changed since the move.

Mum says I should remember that at least I've got Irish Dance class tomorrow, which I'm actually really excited about. I can't wait to meet the teacher and see all the differences between Irish Dance Boston style and Irish Dance – well, Irish style. Lol. Tomorrow's another day and it's bound to be better than today.

Tuesday 2 September

Tuesday should in fact be renamed Disasterday. DIS. AS. TER. Umm. Day.

It started OK. I was so pleased to get to dance class, and the teacher, Mrs Kennedy, seemed OK, a little bit strict maybe but even so she gave me a cool introduction and then the moment I'd been waiting for – she asked me to dance for the class.

I walked up to the front of the class and looked around the room and got my first *really* good look at the other kids. They were all about 10. There was just ONE other girl about my age. Oh well, I thought, maybe some of the others are away or maybe they're just very small for their age. Anyway I was pretty desperate to get back into dancing and it's very unusual for me to turn down the chance to dance. So I pulled up socks and took centre stage (or dance hall). I have to say I think I danced pretty well and people seemed to like it, but then Mrs Kennedy just went off like some kind of mental rocket. Her eyes started flashing and her eyelashes kept opening and shutting really, really fast. She started going on about winning competitions and how dancing like that was *not* how you won competitions. Yeah? Well what about the crate of trophies that are probably stuck in Timbuktu right now that say otherwise, hey? What do *they* say?

5:15 p.m.

I can't believe the way they dance at Mrs Kennedy's dance class. There was this girl Anya and she looked like – well, quite frankly she looked like someone had staple-gunned a plank of wood to either side of her body and made her dance in a very narrow corridor. I don't know what kinda dancing it was, but it sure ain't Irish Dancing Boston style.

Then this really sweet guy from my class followed me out of the class and started telling me how much he liked my dancing. I didn't want to hurt his feelings but he didn't really make it very easy to chat. He just stood there for sooooooooooo long without saying anything. In the end it was so embarrassing I had to look away. Typical, the first person to try to be friends and I had to kinda be a bit rude. I'm going to go in the library for a bit before walking home.

5:23 p.m.
I feel really sad like one of Rory's old soccer balls – all deflated. I started to think, what am I going to do if I can't do Irish Dance? I've done it since I was four, I've *always* done it. I want to MSN Amelia about it, but I don't think she'll really understand and besides when I want to speak to her, she's in class. Charlestown High, Boston, Amelia and Lauren feel a long, long way away right now. I feel really left out of things in Boston but it's not like I've got anything going here. This isn't how I thought it would be, at all. Hopefully things will get much better from now on – I mean it's not like they can get much worse, is it?

6:06 p.m.
Well yes it can. OMG. OMG. Things got MUCH, MUCH worse. I was walking home but I couldn't stop thinking about what my Irish Dance teacher – or Killer Kennedy (as I now think of her) – had said. Then I walked up to the house. I had my key out ready, put the key in the lock no problem, but it wouldn't turn. I kept trying to turn it and it was locked shut. I was desperate to get in the house and kept trying to turn the key. Was pretty panicky at

this point and pretty red-faced, so started shouting 'MUM' through the letterbox and banging on the door pretty loudly. Eventually, after what seemed about ten years, I could see someone behind the glass of the door, and I remember thinking, 'Oh, Rory's a lot taller than he was this morning'.

But THEN the door opens and there's Murphy. Murphy No Second Name. Standing in front of me, while I stand there open-mouthed, red-faced, sweaty hair, saying nothing. I'D ONLY GONE AND GOT THE WRONG HOUSE. No wonder the key wouldn't work – I was trying to get into the house next door to mine. I was trying to get into *Murphy's* house. I have a question for myself: when did I become such a total clown? I could join a circus on recent performance.

Luckily, I had this brilliant idea of making a fantastic recovery by just mumbling something and then running away as fast as I could without saying anything. Maybe he didn't really notice, or maybe he didn't really see who it was. *Who am I kidding?* I thought I heard him laughing as I ran away. What kind of man laughs at someone at the lowest ebb of their young life? I will never ever forgive him. Never.

One other thing I did notice while dangling from the lock is he is much more cute than I noticed on the first day. My powers of perception must be extremely good to have noticed that under such stressful conditions. Maybe I should be a spy!

6:32 p.m.

Wonder if Murphy's on Bebo – might have a quick look – just for research purposes – what is it they say? – know thy enemy. If I knew more about him it would be easy to feel superior to him and never forgive him.

8:30 p.m.

Just spent a quick two hours on Murphy's Bebo site getting evidence. I could have done another half an hour but Rory paid me five euros to get off Dad's computer. So I have news. Guess what? Murphy (Murphy is actually his second name so that's one mystery completely solved) – anyway MURPHY is a dancer, an urban street dancer. We love so many of the same things. It was like SNAP – I love *Step Up* 2 more than *Step Up*, like him, and then SNAP – I love Lupe Fiasco. We have loads in common. His Bebo says he's got this crew and they do all these dance things where they all meet up in really unusual places and bust some moves. Sounds loads of fun but well, it's not very Irish . . . is it? What's the point of being a break dancer in Dublin? That's *got* to be a tough call. He certainly is a curious character, my next-door neighbour.

However, this information changes everything. Oh yes, Mr Murphy, the tables have turned now. Next time I see him I will be quite happy to impart to him my knowledge of the Boston Urban Dance scene as frequented by yours truly at many a Boston underage club. I bet he'd love to see Amelia's snake. Hey maybe she can put it on YouTube and I can show him. When he hears all about my knowledge about his subject he'll forget all about 'that door incident' and see me for the sophisticate I really am.

JUST MURPHY

Friday 5 September

And today's question is: how could I have got it so wrong? Again! So I see Murphy and his crew. So, I go up to him and his mates, airily dismiss yesterday's embarrassing incident and ask him if he wants to go for a soda sometime. What's wrong with that? Cue Long Pause. Cue tumbleweed rolling across the playground. You'd think I was Angelina Jolie trying to get off with Brad Pitt on the set of *Mr and Mrs Smith*. Suddenly the Wicked Witches of the East and West (Eavanne and Sorcha) appear by broomstick and – what a surprise – everyone's laughing at me all over again because I thought Murphy and I might go for a soda? I'm beginning to wonder just what you have to do in this country to *not* be laughed at by everyone?

So that girl from the other day Siobhan took me back to her parents' place, they are mad crazy about backgammon and are away all the time competing. Siobhan's actually kind of cool and it was a little bit like hanging out with Amelia. Talking of which, I'm still waiting for MSN contact.

But in the meantime, Siobhan really helped me with something I was struggling to understand. Finally: Dating

Dublin Style, a handy cut-out-and-keep guide to the DOs and the DON'Ts.

Here are the DON'Ts.

1. Guys and girls DON'T hang out together in Ireland.
2. They DON'T date. No soda. No study dates. No bowling. No Ball Games.

And here is what you can DO.

1. You DO just go out with each other but without actually going out anywhere.
2. You DO occasionally have a snog.
3. Umm. That's it.
4. What?

So Siobhan told me that once upon a thousand years ago Eavanne and Murphy had a snog and now Eavanne reckons they're going out – although they're not – and gets really jealous if he talks to any other girls.

Yes. Because that all makes perfect sense. Not. What am I going to do? Every day it's more confusing. One thing I do know though: Eavanne can't stop Murphy and I being friends. I mean, you just can't decide you're going out with someone and therefore control who they're friends with, can you? That would be mental.

Wednesday 10 September

I was online again looking at Murphy's Bebo profile. Under relationship status it says 'It's Complicated'. Ye-es, it certainly is when you're forced to go out with someone you're not even going out with. Interesting that Eavanne's reads 'Seeing Someone' – how lame is that? I suppose she could say she is actually seeing someone as in she does actually SEE Murphy.

Wait. Finally. Joy of joys – Amelia (MEL) is online.

AIS: Mel!!!!!!!!!!!!!!!

MEL: Ais. How r u? We get 2 chat!

AIS: Yay. How's every1 at Irish Dance?

MEL: Fine. We miss u. Regionals in 1 wk. Soooooooooooo much 2 do.

AIS: Wow. I wish I was 2 and not forced 2 attend Mrs Kennedy's School of Irish Hell . . . I mean Dancing.

MEL: You tooooooooooooooooo funny.

AIS: And – she blushes – how's the gorgeous Phil Donnelly?

MEL: ☺

AIS: ☺?

MEL: Well . . .

AIS: Not with Tinker Bell?

MEL: No, not Tinker Bell.

AIS: But . . .??????????????

MEL: Ais, Woody said Phil's going 2 ask Colleen 2 the formal.

AIS: Oh no. OH NO. OH NO.

MEL: U OK?

AIS: Yeah.

MEL: Really?

AIS: Sure? Promise.

MEL: She was gonna email u about it. I said she should.

AIS: Thanks, Mel.

MEL: Ur not cross with me r u?

AIS: No. Course not.

6:01 p.m.
He's gonna ask Colleen out to the formal?

6:03 p.m.
Went downstairs to get some food, but there was only fruit. When will those in charge of shopping understand that a teenager in crisis cannot survive on fruit alone? Does no one in Ireland *like* snacks? Ah, what I would do for a big handful of goldfish crackers. While I padded round the kitchen looking for something other than apricots to eat, like some kind of tiger on the look-out for a tasty gazelle, Aunty Stella continued to talk for Ireland. If talking was an Olympic sport, Aunty Stell would have won gold for Ireland in Beijing 2008, no worries.

Stella said she was having her kitchen totally redone. It's costing 20,000 euros! I reckon she could get one for half that and donate the rest of the money to a donkey sanctuary. She kept going on about her new kitchen, Mum said later she thinks the whole reason Aunty Stella came over was to tell us how much the kitchen cost. Why would she do that though? It must be a pretty amazing kitchen if she's going round people's houses to tell them about it. She was also going on about where we live, apparently it's quite a nice area but not the best area to live in. That is D4, which is where she lives. Doesn't sound that great to me, sounds like some kind of military training camp. I wasn't really listening to all this boring adult chat. For a start I was teetering, as I was on the brink of starvation, and had just experienced a massive emotional crisis.

However, in order to be polite I kept one ear on the conversation, AND THANK GOD I DID otherwise I would have missed the really interesting bit. She also said. WAIT FOR IT. That there's this guy on our estate who's kind of a real 'bad boy'. Apparently he hangs out with a group of *degenerates* (had to look up this word, it's always quite hard to understand when Aunt Stella comes over – it means *troublemakers*). What? And then I realized the Bad Boy she was talking about was my Murphy. And the troublemakers, that must be his crew. Wait, she can't be talking about that group of twerps I saw yesterday, can she? Clutching hold of the box of dried apricots, I tried to listen closely.

This is definitely all true, because Aunty Stella's hairdresser (Denise) does Murphy's mum's waxing and Denise had said that Murphy's mum was really worried about Murphy getting into trouble with the police since he's got in with his crew. Well, lady, they sure didn't look like a gang to me. They looked like a load of wimpy Irish boys trying to look like rap stars in their baggy trousers and gold chains. They should see some of the people Amelia and I used to see at Urban Dance class if they want to see what degenerates *really* look like. Why are adults always so taken in by people's clothes? Dad always used to grip the steering wheel more firmly when he saw some of the kids at the day discos in their big baggy trousers, baseball hats and P Diddy leisurewear – that's probably because he didn't see them like I did – going into a massive sulk just because they can't spin the helicopter as well as their mate.

8:10 p.m.
No email from that snake Colleen. Can't believe she's going to even *think* about going to formal with Phil. I mean, yes, OK, there are a few problems with us getting together, like being on separate continents, but there's a principle involved here, isn't there?

8:12 p.m.
And then there's Murphy. Ahh, Murphy! He makes Phil Donnelly look like a four on the scale of gorgeousness. Ah, in that case maybe Colleen can have Phil? What am I *thinking*, no *way* – I've been into Phil Donnelly since first grade. No way, Colleen.

8:14 p.m.
When will it end? So now, Mum had to go round Aunty Stella's to look at her kitchen. She said she was going to go and 'get it over with'. I was trying to work in my room. I couldn't MSN Amelia because she was back in class. The time difference really sucks. I just couldn't work

– James Joyce may as well be written in Arabic for all the sense I can make of it.

So, I went downstairs with James Joyce (the book, not the person) and found Dad sitting on the couch reading a copy of *Plumbing Monthly*. He was reading an article on rainwater tanks, which he said was written really badly. He said he has to read up about it all now he's back in Ireland working for his brother. Imagine *that*, imagine you think you've finished with James Joyce FOREVER and then ten years later you find out you've got to read it all over again. Argghhhh. Poor Dad! We watched telly for a bit together. Guess what it was? *Father Ted*.

Monday 15 September

OK so firstly Kennedy is just like a total horror show to everyone. This poor girl Mushira was trying to do the first couple of moves in this step dance, and she just couldn't get it. Killer Kennedy was shouting at her in Irish, and was making the poor girl really nervous. In the end she turned the music off and I thought she was going to rocket off again like she did at me before, but Mushira stood up straight just like Kennedy wanted and managed to avoid a big shout-athon. Seeing Kennedy calm down a bit was great but I knew Mushira still hadn't got it. So I showed her the way we did it Charlestown style. She nearly got it but Kennedy was beginning to go a bit red faced again so I decided to leave it there before her eyelashes started flashing together.

As we were leaving, Murphy and his band of degenerates

(ha!) were coming into the room. They had a big boom box, Murphy looked pretty shocked to see me. I just pushed past him but he shouted after me 'Hey Miss USA, what you up to?' I told him: 'Irish Dancing', and he just started laughing. I gave him my Aisling Hard Stare though and he soon shut up. I decided to let him know I was not impressed with the way his so-called mates had treated me the other day. And he did apologize on their behalf. HA!

Then it turns out that he's been watching Rory and me dancing in the garden!! All those goofy moves we were doing – how embarrassing is that? Is *nothing* sacred? *Is a girl no longer allowed to practise her moves in the garden without fear of being watched?* I thought indignantly, then I thought: *I do hope I was wearing my cool stripy orange T-shirt when he was spying on me.*

Then he started going on about Guru and Gang Starr. I was like, what does an Irish guy know about US Hip Hop? He got REALLY annoyed at that point. But before I could apologize, guess who turns up like a bad smell? Only Little Miss Limpet, Eavanne. She walked right up to him, put her arm through his, called ME a loser and walked Murphy away from me. I wanted to shout: 'You're Not Even Going Out With Him, You Freak. Who's the loser now?' But I didn't think about it until about two hours later and I didn't know where they'd gone. Murphy. Please write this on a post-it and put it on your bathroom mirror to remind yourself: 'I, Murphy, am NOT going out with Eavanne'.

8:02 p.m.

To: Aisling Fitzsimons
From: Colleen McLaughlin
Subject: Hi

Dear Aisling. How r u? Wot u been up to? We won the State Regionals. We really missed you tho. Phil wants me to go to school Formal with him. Would that be OK, I know you kinda liked him. Colleen.
PS Phil's here. He says 'Hi, Fitzsimons, how's Ireland?'

8:03 p.m.
So an email from the snake. I can't believe I lent her my spare hairpiece in the regionals last year when hers got burnt when her mum left the curling irons on it for too long. I wish I never had. I wish I'd left her to her own wispy badly curled hair and never helped her.

I would never try for a man if someone else was interested in him. What happened to the sisterhood?

8:04 p.m.
Unless it was Eavanne. Eavanne isn't part of the sisterhood.

Wednesday 17 September

Irish Dancing lessons should be just renamed Irish Shouting lessons, because I sure have to listen to a lot more shouting than I do dancing. Another dancing lesson; another lesson in Gaelic shouting. How come the only words I know how to say in Gaelic are 'will you please try to keep your arms by your side'? That's sure going to come in handy, isn't it? I wonder what career options that grasp of the Irish language is going to open up for me. Maybe a Sergeant Major – hey, maybe Mrs Kennedy is ex army. Then things would make sense. I bet her friends call her Killer Kennedy or KK for short.

It doesn't seem to matter what I do or how hard I try, I can't please KK. I try to do it her way, I *really* do, but it's so stiff and difficult. I concentrate on what she's saying but then I notice my arms are suddenly moving around a bit like I've gone all Mr Tickle or I'll suddenly find myself moving to a different rhythm in the music. Of course that's the moment old Killer Kennedy has chosen to stand right in front of me watching me like a HAWK.

Sometimes I can't help but think that I don't fit in because I'm too old to do Irish Dance – the only kids who do this kind of dance here are the real young ones. It's like every kid in Ireland does it at first, but by the time everyone's reached twelve they've stopped. That explains why there's no Irish Dance gang, because no one does it. At the moment it's looking, to the detective in me, like the big problem IS the Irish Dance itself. Maybe I should give it up? But Mum would go mental. And if I did, then what would I have left? I wish someone would just tell me where I fit in and then I could just go and get on with it.

When I feel like this, I can't help myself from wishing that Dad had never lost his job and decided to move us all back to Ireland. Because if he hadn't I'd still have loads of friends and everything would be fine. I wish I could wake up tomorrow and I'd be in Charlestown and going to school with Amelia and Lauren. Even Colleen!

Come on, Aisling. Pull yourself together.

6:58 p.m.
Have just remembered, there is of course one HUGE upside to this. This upside has a number of key characteristics: it can be found riding along the country roads of Ireland on a Vespa, it has dark hair and is kind of boy-shaped and is known as a lesser spotted Murphy.

7:01 p.m.
News flash! Mum saw straight through my attempt to keep my composure. How does she *do* that? Eventually, I had no choice but to tell her everything. She says it's been hard for her too. I guess I never thought that she might be missing her friends too, I only saw it from what I was missing. Mum was really cool and said if I keep making an effort for a few more weeks, and keep on trying to make the best of Irish Dance class, she'll try to see if they could afford a ticket for me to go back to Boston. A plane ticket home to Boston!!! This is the best news *ever*.

This would mean I could be back in Boston in less than six weeks, 42 days. Woop woop.

SCHOOL PROJECT

Monday 22 September

Transition Year Project. Ex-squeeze me? A 'whatsition' year project? Here is the general idea, as I understand it, and I ain't no expert. So, we have to work as a group on a project to come up with a business idea and then go out and set up said business so we can learn how to make some folding money. Hey, I sound like Rory!

Deep down I know this is all a scam from the Irish government so we:

1. Learn how to be self-sufficient (and so don't end up on welfare sitting in front of daytime TV eating cereal from a box).
2. Go out and do something with our lives and win 'Irish Business Woman of the Year' nominations.

I'm in Group C and thankfully so is that sweet guy from Irish Dance, Ali, and Siobhan – the one who told me about Eavanne and Murphy (not that there *is* an Eavanne and Murphy, right?). I said to Siobhan we were in the group together and she just smiled. Every time I think we're becoming really good friends, I just don't know – I think she likes me. Anyway, it doesn't matter because at least for the first time since I arrived in Ireland I'm in a gang – even if it took a teacher to put me in it! I guess you could say I'm in the kind of 'geek and sweet' gang. Trouble is, we three – sweet, geek and bad Irish Dancer – have no idea what to do. Nothing Nada Niente. As soon as Miss O'Connor announced the project Eavanne said, 'Ooh I've been waiting for two years for this.' Apparently, Sorcha and her are going to make a fashion magazine, they even have a name for it: *Pulse*. Oh purlease, I thought, who's going to be interested in THAT? But Ali immediately started nodding in their general direction and said, that sounds like a good idea, and I had to once again resort to my Aisling Hard Stare.

At Charlestown High they would give us loads of ideas to work with. I was explaining this to Siobhan but she just shot me this look and said, 'So you need to be told what to do, do you?' Ouch! She's right tho', sixteen is totally time enough to start thinking about sorting things out for yourself. Well, I'm ready for a challenge.

3:54 p.m.

OMG. I was walking back from school when I could hear someone following me. I turned round and saw Murphy. I kept on walking, refusing to be impressed by his little scooter, when he stopped beside me. He just handed me his spare helmet as if I'd grab it and put it on. 'Quick, get on,' he said. I was just about to tell him to 'Get Lost'. But just then I saw Aunty Stella's car coming round the corner towards our house and I had this sudden vision of me sitting at home listening to her going on about how solid oak worktops are the best. So, before I knew it, I'd hopped on the back, and had my arms wrapped around the very fit Murphy. Amelia is going to go crazy when I tell her this. But that's not the best bit. The best bit was we saw one half of *Pulse*'s editorial team, the one and only Sorcha McFadden. Zoom we went, right past her, Zoom Zoom Zoom. I grinned widely and saw her reach for her mobile. Would love to have been there when Eavanne gets *that* text. Print *that* in your magazine, lady.

As we were riding along I had to hold really tightly on to Murphy. Although at one point he had to stop his Vespa to ask me to loosen my grip a little bit because it was actually stopping him from being able to breathe. Which makes him a bit of a moaner when you think that he's the one who told me to hold on tightly in the first place.

4:35 p.m.
Beginning to wonder what I'm doing here. Murphy practically ran off as soon as we got here. And I don't know anyone else. All of his crew are here but they look pretty different out of school. Maybe Stella is right and they *are* troublemakers. I wish I was at home with Mum and Aunty Stell and a big plate of fish-fingers.

4:36 p.m.
Pull yourself together, Aisling Fitzsimons – you are not scared of a couple of idiots in B Ape Baseball caps. That's not even a real baseball team, I don't think.

4:38 p.m.

Murphy just gave me the biggest smile in the Northern Hemisphere. Now everything is OK.

4:48 p.m.

OK, people. Finally I get it. The plan is they do some pretty spectacular dance moves here, kinda on location. Upload them to this specialist site and BINGO. Top prize is to dance in an Ace FX video. Cool! Although, who would have thought Irish lads like these would want to even *do* that?

4:51 p.m.

Murphy does not look happy. They've had a dress rehearsal (umm, don't think that's what it's called) and Murphy's given his crew this kind of half-time talk, said they're gonna have to do much better to be in the Ace FX video.

I heard him say to Dec that they needed to raise the stakes, or get a 'secret weapon' to beat the Fat Playaz. Murphy said to Dec that he didn't think his dancing was up to it. I wanted to shout, 'You don't understand, you're the best dancer I've ever seen, I'd never seen a white kid flip from a standing start before, Murphy – you can MOOOOOVE', but I decided just to sit quietly and think it instead.

4:55 p.m.

Everyone's dancing except me. It's a struggle not to jump up, grab Murphy by the hand and really DANCE like I

Aislings Diary

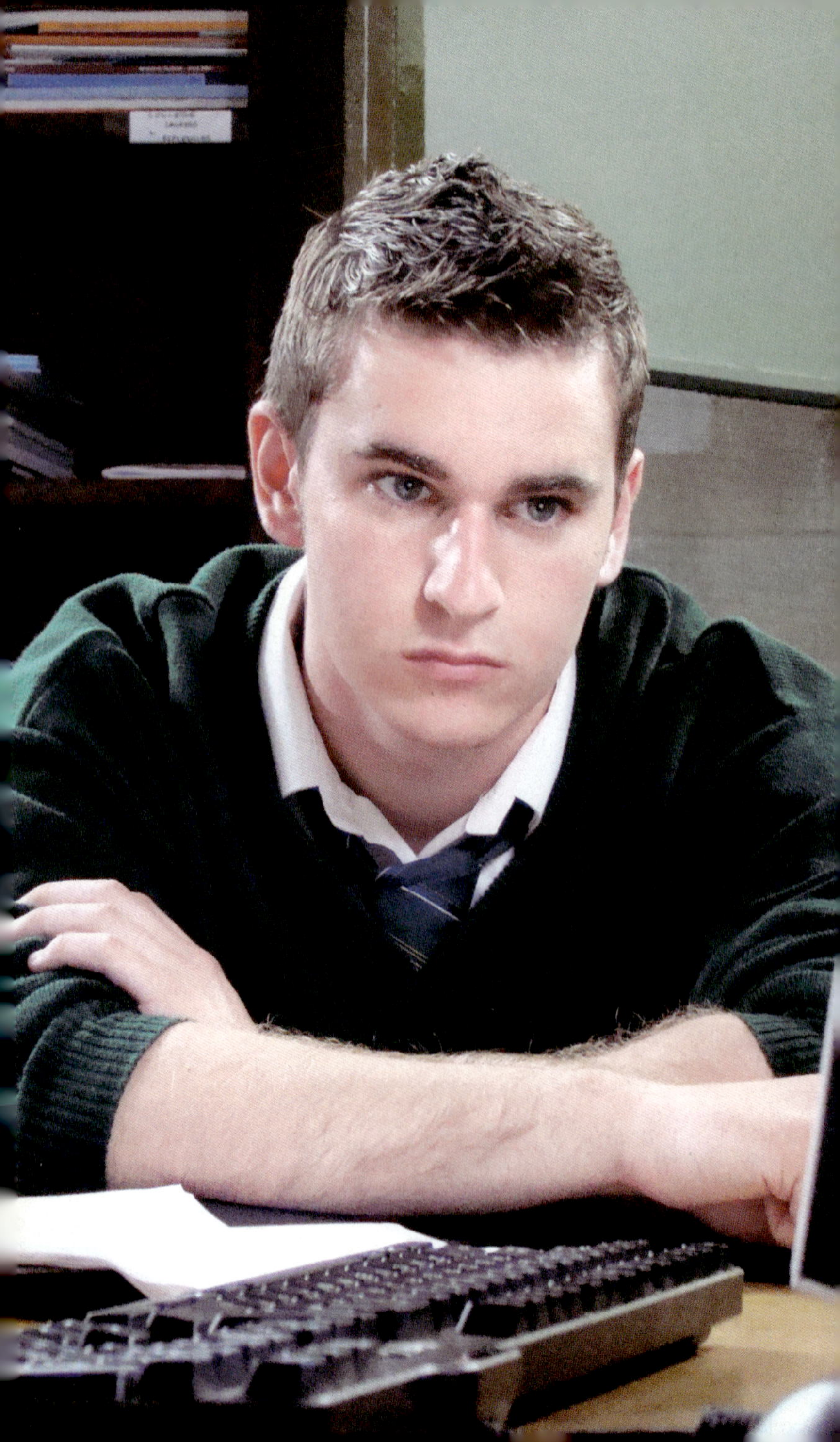

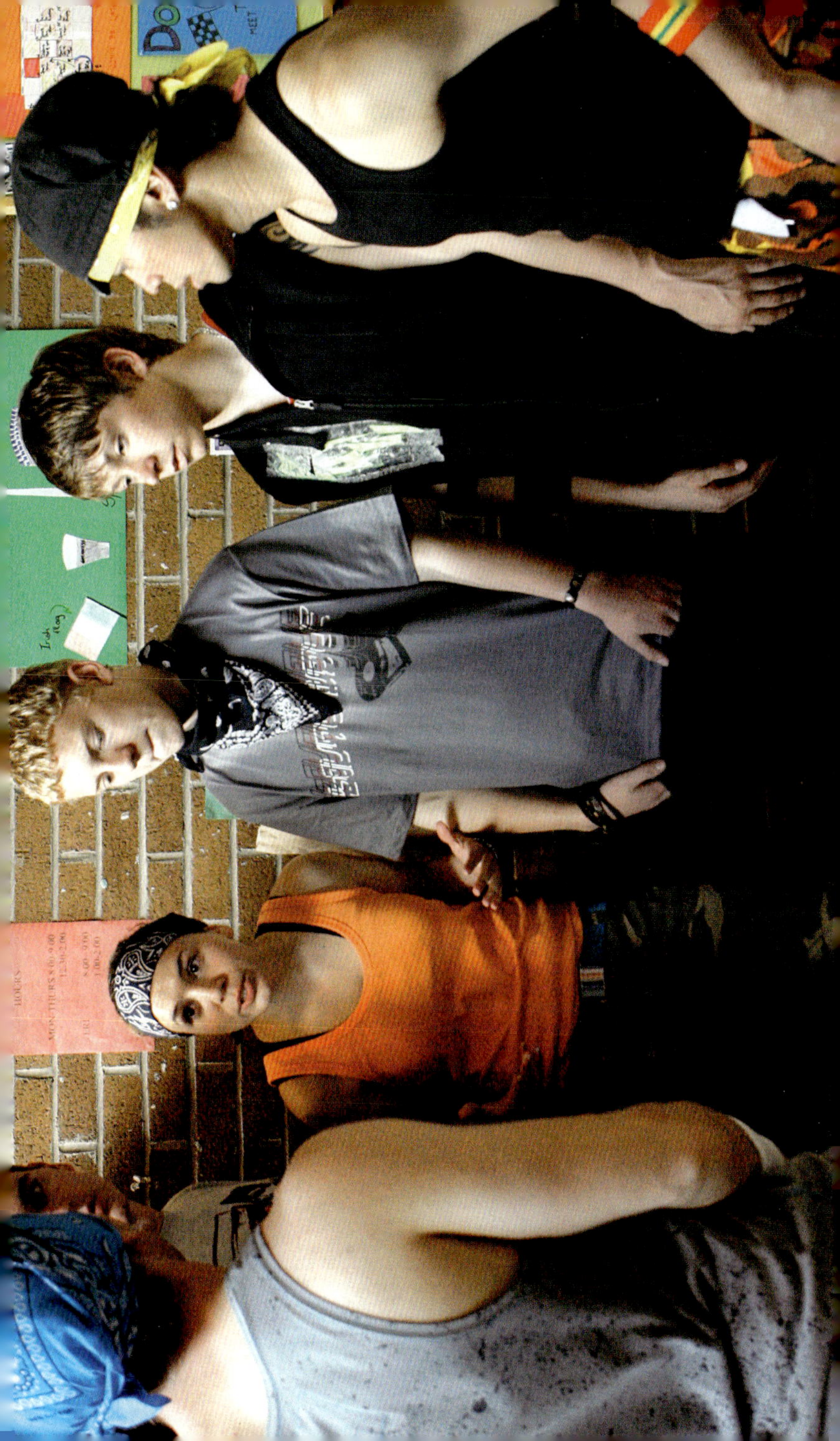

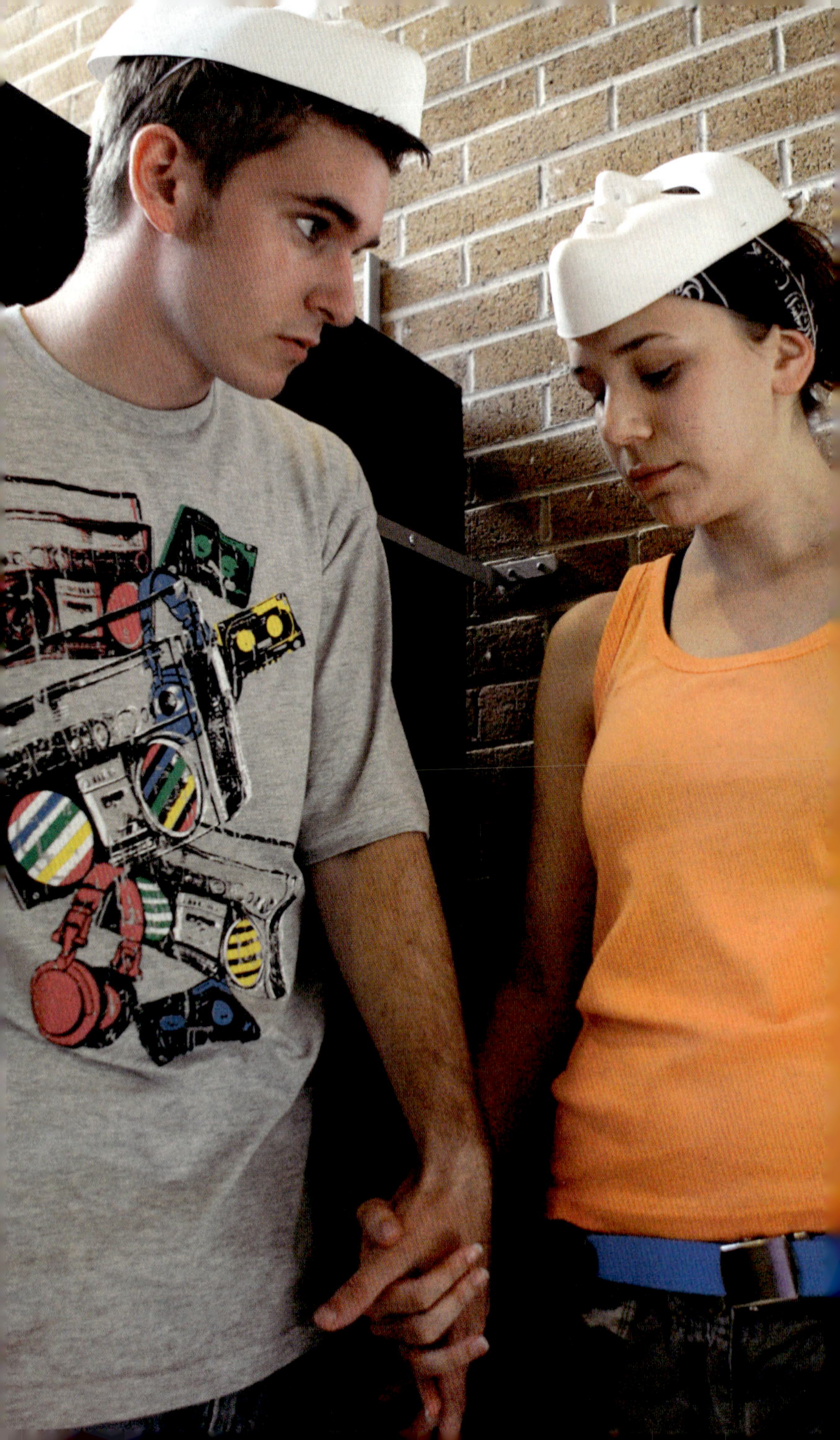

really want to. I can't though, not in front of his knucklehead crew. I couldn't really see HOW they were doing what they were doing. It was kinda break-dancing but not really anything Amelia and I had tried before. I didn't want to get it all wrong and have everyone laugh at me. JP must have seen me watching them because he shouted: 'She can't do it without her batters'.

I heard everyone laughing and I looked up at Murphy but he wasn't – he actually looked really concerned about me. Then, I realized how stupid I was being, I just *knew* I could do better than all of them. I remembered Mrs Kennedy's class and how awful it was dancing in front of them and I thought *You know what? I can dance*. And then suddenly I was standing there in front of Murphy. And the music was playing, and the music filled me, and then I just started dancing. At first it felt brilliant, the fresh air – I did a couple of moves to the music, I was actually enjoying myself. Then Murphy showed me this sequence, I thought I could do it but it messed up. I just couldn't get it right. What a surprise! Something else I couldn't do properly. I tried again and properly messed up. I looked over to JP to give him an Aisling Hard Stare for laughing but he wasn't laughing, he was trying the move too. AND NOT EVEN HE COULD DO IT. I thought *This is madness* – they *can't even get it right and these are* their *moves, what hope have* I *got?*

Definitely time to leave, I thought, but Murphy stopped me (which is just as well given I had no idea where I was at all). I said to him 'There's no point in carrying on, I'm not doing it right' but he said, 'There is no right'. And then I realized – yeah – they didn't really have any rules, they were just trying stuff out. Cool. So I tried his move again but not quite the way he did. It kinda worked. It was this freaky move, part break, part Irish Dancing. Some mad old fusion of styles. I looked up to see if everyone was laughing but they weren't, they were all just kind of staring at me. I shouted, 'Quit staring', but Dec said, 'This girl is good', and even JP the knucklehead was impressed. I did some more of my dancing and on one of the moves Murphy held my hand. This isn't France, friends don't hold hands – this is Ireland, holding hands *means* something. I just don't know what.

Tuesday 23 September

So this is the perfect time to rework the best days of my romantic life (so far) because there are two new entries – an unprecedented event since the list was created in first grade.

1. (new entry) Today – HOLDING HANDS WITH MURPHY.
2. (down from 1) Phil Donnelly coming to find me backstage of the show to say bye.
3. (up from 5) Adam Wiltshire buying me some Swizzlers at the School Summer Fair.
4. (down from 2) Billie Byrne giving me that note saying Phil Donnelly fancies me.
5. (new entry) Seeing Murphy on his scooter for the first time.

10:07 p.m.

Can't sleep, keep thinking about having my arms round Murphy on the back of his scooter. It's hard to sleep when you keep thinking about dancing at a disused bridge with your next-door neighbour, I am finding.

10:09 p.m.

Wonder if Eavanne is still reading that text. Ha ha ha ha ha. Got you back – perhaps it will help you remember not to mess with the best.

Thursday 25 September

KK was on the warpath today. Class was really hard. I've been reworking the steps I did with Murphy so much I was so tired by the time I got to the dance work camp (as I've come to think of Mrs Kennedy's dance class).

I've got my first competition the weekend after next!! Argghhh.

Killer Kennedy wants us to practise all the hours possible for then. I should at least place if I spend every single spare moment of every day trying to dance Killer Kennedy style. Mum's really excited about the competition and is expecting me to 'knock 'em down' as she calls it. I haven't seen her that excited about anything for ages. I haven't the heart to tell her that I find this kind of dancing about as exciting as watching cousin Shane pick his nose, i.e. not very.

And now just what you've been waiting for, today's MURPHY NEWS ROUND-UP:

As I was leaving dance class Ali was asking me if I'd

had any thoughts about our company thing. I had completely forgot about it. We were gonna go and grab a coffee but then Murphy appeared looking off the scale in terms of general gorgeousness and hitching a ride straight into cutesville. Anyway he offered me a lift home on el vesperama, as they say in Italy. It was great, although unfortunately we didn't see any of the *Pulse* Editorial Team. Must remember to change my romantic list to reflect this new development.

4:05 p.m.

Murphy's asked me to dance with his crew next week on Wednesday!!!!!! I can't of course because I have Irish Dancing. And I am already way, way behind schedule for the Irish Dance competition. But he said he thought I was good. Really good. When I said I had Irish Dance class the same night, he got that look again like when I said I didn't know the Irish could break-dance. He said, 'You don't have to do what you've always done, it's OK to do new things.' Then he zoomed off on his scooter, leaving me standing there a bit open-mouthed – like Sorcha the other day. This is not so good.

4:32 p.m.

Trying to remember the last time Irish Dancing was new and exciting. It seems like it was a long time ago.

4:54 p.m.

So Mum is having a complete nervy-b about me being on a motorbike. I was like, 'MUM, it's more of a moped than a motorbike'. Dad got all wistful and said when things 'got a bit easier' he was going to get another motorbike but then Mum gave him a look which is very like my Aisling Hard Stare. Dad then completely shut up about getting his own bike. It was too late for Mum though, she went completely mental (almost on the scale of Killer Kennedy) and said I can't go on Murphy's scooter any more. How unfair is *that*? Hanging out with Murphy is the only fun I've had since we got to stupid Ireland and now I'm not allowed to do it any more because old new-kitchen bore Aunty Stella thinks the knuckleheads are some kind of threat to the establishment because they like urban music and wear ridiculous trousers. What kind of world are they *living* in? This is unfair. Unfair, unfair, unfair, unfair, unfair x 1,000,000.

Friday 26 September

Outside I shall be calm and cool and collected, inside I am seething with injustice of the situation, like the Dalai Lama and Tibet.

Eventually my façade cracked in the school toilets and I was forced to let the torrent of emotion spill out to Siobhan. She was pretty much the nicest anyone has been to me since I've been in Dublin, despite technically siding with Mum over the motorbike (NOT A MOTORBIKE) issue. It's making me think, does ANYBODY in the whole of Ireland actually know the difference between a motorbike and a Vespa? One is a massive engine that middle-aged men buy in a crisis so they can dress in leather and look younger AND the other is a cool, quick, environmentally friendly method of transport driven by cool dudes and their dudettes (yuck).

However, Siobhan seemed to know all about Murphy asking me out (NOT asking me out, but asking me to dance with the crew). She said it's called flashmobbing. I did that thing where you pretend you know what's going on, and sort of agreed, but inside I was saying, 'what's *flashmobbing*'?

3:55 p.m.

Just looked up flashmobbing on Wikipedia. All it said was that it was just people meeting up to dance – sounds pretty harmless to me. Rory came by while I was looking at the computer on his rollerblades (not *inside*, Rory, how many *more* times) – he shouted 'Flashmobbing, how cool is that? Who's going flashmobbing, sis?' I of course had to ask him what he knew about it. 'I know it's cool' was the answer I got. Ah well, if you ask an idiot a question . . .

4:23 p.m.

Just texted Murphy. 'Are we flashmobbing?' Got one straight back: 'Are you asking? M'.

4:25 p.m.

Well what does *that* mean? I'm beginning to understand it now when Mum scrunches her nose up and says 'Men!' after Dad has done something particularly annoying. Men!

4:28 p.m.

Here are some facts. Fact numero uno, I can't take any time off from practising for the Irish Dance competition because I'm already favourite to come last. And how much would Killer Kennedy like that? So Irish Dance practice has to be my number one priority, right now. Fact number two: flashmobbing with Murphy is about as high up my list of priorities as it's possible to go though. Houston – we have a problem, I have two number-one priorities.

5:36 p.m.

Siobhan has a solution. She listened to me all the way through looking straight at me, like she does, and then said simply: 'Why don't you just ditch the Irish Dancing and go to the flashmob if that's what you want to do?' How could I? Irish Dancing is what I do, what I've always done, it's who I *am*. If I don't have that I don't have anything. I gave her the little speech that my teacher in Boston used to say about our Irish heritage but Siobhan shrugged and said that Ireland was full of so many influences now that Irish Dance was just part of it. But I don't agree, she doesn't know what being Irish in Boston means. Irish Dance is my heritage, my family, it's who I *am*. There's no way I can give up Irish Dance, even if I really wanted to, even if it meant I got to go out with Murphy, because . . . well, because . . . because Mum would kill me for one thing.

Monday 29 September

One week after we were given our Transition Year Project and Team C still have no idea what to do WHATSOEVER. Ali the Geek said that his Dad wanted him to do something with the hospital – maybe set up a volunteer programme. Brilliant, I thought, but then he admitted that the sight of blood made him sick as a dog. So that was that for *that* idea. Then Siobhan suggested a mobile manicure service, which sounded great until we thought of giving people pedicures. Yuck. Then we saw a load of kids with face paints go by on the way to a party and then we had the Idea of the Century. Da dah. We're gonna do children's parties, we're gonna do children's parties. We're gonna party like it's your children's birthday, yeah we're gonna party like it's your children's birthday.

THAT'S MAGIC

Wednesday 1 October

So today we did the big pitch of our Transition Year Projects. I saw old plastic not-so-fantastic Eavanne copying ideas from a magazine. What a swizz. She's just a big ol' CHEAT!! Then, when teach looked at her she slid it back into her bag. So basically her big idea from two years ago was to copy stuff out of a magazine. Her parents must be soooooo proud. We're up next.

11:20 a.m.

Everyone loved our idea and we decided to have our first meeting tonight at four-thirty to discuss.

Just seen Murphy and he asked me again to go dancing with him later. What a bummer. I really want to go but I have a meeting planned with Ali and Siobhan AND dance class. But I really want to go. I wish I could be in two places at once and then everyone would be happy.

3:32 p.m.

Revelation. Have worked out I can just do both – if I get a lift back to meet Ali and Siobhan on M's Vespa. Hooray for the Vespa. It's almost as good as Dr Who's Tardis. Unless you're Mum in which case it's the most dangerous thing on the planet, more dangerous than nuclear bombs or hiding the remote from Dad when the football's on. I know she said I technically couldn't go on it – but – here's the magic bit. She doesn't have to know. It's not lying. No siree bob. No, it's being *economical with the truth*. That's a different thing completely. I have to go on the scooter or there's no way I can do the Murphy dance AND meet Siobhan and Ali, because Siobhan is not keen on waiting around for people, so I have no choice. It's Vespa or bust for me.

4:30 p.m.

The dance thing was a-maz-ing – I danced with Murphy and loads of people were standing round and looking at us – we got quite a crowd. It felt so good being able to dance with him, so different to Irish Dance class – well, for a start I was allowed to move my arms.

4:34 p.m.
And breathe. I made it to the meeting only a fraction late. I don't know how much Siobhan's eyes would have rolled at me if I hadn't got a lift on Murphy's Vespa. But it was all OK, we have now formalized Parties-to-Go and I am technically running my own business.

We have come up with a list of things that need to be done to get Parties-to-Go up and going:

1. Put flyers up in the mall.
2. Ask around for people who need top-notch children's party planners.
3. Make loads of money, get an A and beat the Wicked Witches of the West and East, as I've started to think of Eavanne and Sorcha.

Ali went all weird again when his dad turned up. Mr Ali didn't come in and looked really stern in a big silver car outside the café until Ali left. Glad he's not *my dad*.

Friday 3 October
Hey, guess what? A friend of a friend of Siobhan's mum got us an interview for Parties-to-Go with Mrs Griffin and her daughter Chelsea who's turning six and wants to party. For your entertainment I thought I would make

you a brief list of things Chelsea and Chelsea's mum need to make it the party of the year . . .

1. Magician, one
2. Karaoke machine, one
3. Make-up artist, one
4. A Ferris wheel, one
5. Face painting, face paints and someone to put them on
6. Haunted house, one
7. Hummer limo, just the one! Luckily!

That's easy then. We'll just go down the haunted magic musical paint and pet shop and pick those things up. 'Oh and grab us one of those Ferris wheels from out the back, will you? What's that, you're out of Hummer limos, oh what a shame.' What *is* the deal with these Dublin mums and their children's parties? In Boston you're lucky to get a balloon, a piece of novelty cake and one of your friends temporarily sawn in half.

Not complaining though. If Parties-to-Go can pull it off we're gonna ace the Transition Year Project. Chelsea had faith in us though – we're booked for this weekend. Parties-to-Go has officially got going. Wonder how *Pulse* is doing. Not. Lol.

6:02 p.m.

Just got back from the Non-Stop Party Shop, although it didn't feel like much of a party in there, especially when you were paying at the checkout. I bet their party spirit would quickly disappear if you couldn't pay. Ha ha. Anyway we got tattoos (washable ones – I don't think the Dublin Mum Brigade would like it if we did real ones lol), stickers, puppets and a book on face painting. Ali saw this magic set and made us get it. It looks really complicated. Who knows *what* we're going to do with that? I should really make a list of everything we need to do for Saturday but instead I'm going to paint my friend Siobhan's face so she looks like a tiger. Grrrr.

6:16 p.m.

Siobhan thinks she looks like a tiger but I think I've kind of made her look stripy. I suppose tigers *are* stripy. It's nothing that can't be perfected with a whole load of practice. By Saturday I will be the best Tiger Face Painter in the whole of Dublin. Of that I promise you.

7:16 p.m.

All I said to Ali was 'Stay there, I want to have a go at turning you into a butterfly face' and he just disappeared. I know he's supposed to be this genius magician but I didn't know he could literally disappear into thin air. However, using my incredible powers of perception (and my ears) I managed to trace him and my dad to the shed. I also noticed that there was a load of face glitter, the magic set and some of the crates from the move missing. Ali was in the shed for a very long time and I heard loads of sawing and I think what sounded like 'Da dah!' I wonder if he is up to no good. When I asked him afterwards he said 'wait and see', then I asked Siobhan and she said 'who knows' and then when I asked Dad later he said, 'Aisling, why don't you wait and see'. How would they like it if I just went around telling everyone to wait and see?

Saturday 4 October
1:00 p.m.
Just got back from the dancing competition. What can I say? Well, here are a few words to describe it: waiting, boring, dancing, shouting, disappointment, waiting, watching, other people getting prizes, driving home. The truth is, Mrs Kennedy is right. I suck! No time to dwell. Lunch – hope Rory keeps his mouth shut and doesn't keep going on about how much I sucked.

3:01 p.m.
Parties-to-Go start their business today. Just about to leave to go and meet Ali. I've just had a very worrying thought. What do I know about kids? What does any of Group C know about kids' parties? Arghhh. Perhaps if I hide in my bedroom I won't have to go and entertain thirty six-year-olds. Oh no, there's the doorbell, it's Siobhan. Gulp. I've got to go.

3:45 p.m.
Siobhan and I have just finished decorating the house. She wanted to do the house and for me to do the garden, but that seemed crazy because it would be much quicker doing

both together. She really didn't want to do it together, but in a while we really got a rhythm goin' on. It looks great.

We had these helium balloons – if you breathe in a little bit of the air from one of the balloons it makes your voice go all funny – I kept saying 'Siobhan, would you mind telling me about the main themes in James Joyce' like Mrs C the English teacher and she was really laughing. We had to stop when Mrs Griffin came in because we are, of course, professionals but I could see Siobhan was laughing so much she couldn't even look me in the eye and had to concentrate very hard on putting the balloons up.

All we have to do now is wait for the kids to show up so they can tear down all our decorations and we can try to stop them breathing in the helium balloons. Fun!

3:50 p.m.
The first kid has arrived. He's dressed as Spiderman – I think his costume is better than Tobey Maguire's himself – it's a perfect replica! How much must have *that* cost?

3:56 p.m.
Time, I think, to break out the old face paints. Unfortunately, I'm not as good as I thought at the Butterfly Face – mentioning no names, Ali, but I'm not one to hold a grudge. Let's get this party started.

4:35 p.m.
Mixed success with the face paints. I've got to be honest. I hadn't exactly got round to doing the twenty practice

tigers the book told you to do. And it wasn't quite as easy on the kid as when I was practising on Siobhan, as she actually sat still and wasn't trying to eat a big bowl of ice cream at the same time.

Even when I'd done my best job it was clear to everyone who's ever seen the Discovery Channel that he didn't look like a tiger at all. He looked like an orange and black stripy-faced kid. Mrs Griffin was not happy. She said, 'And what type of tiger is *that*, Aisling Fitzsimons?' in this really funny voice. The kid looked like he was going to cry and I thought it was curtains for Parties-to-Go. But then Siobhan said 'He's a Celtic Tiger, Mrs Griffin.' Then I started doing this funky dance. Singing 'Ooh ooh I'm a dancing tiger' with a couple of break moves and a big roar at the end. Then the stripy kid started shouting 'Ooh, ooh, I'm a dancing tiger', then suddenly a couple of kids near us started shouting 'Us too' and then they all made me do the same thing to them. Gotta go – there is a line of FIVE kids awaiting my face-painting skills. FIVE. Count 'em.

4:56 p.m.
If I ever see any type of wild cat again in my life it will be *way* too soon. I didn't even think Ireland *had* any tigers. Maybe it had in olden times.

4:58 p.m.
Mrs Griffin has thankfully put a pair of furry cat ears on Chelsea's head – which gives a kind of clue as to what she's supposed to be. Great. This might also help with

the parents working out why their perfectly fresh-faced youngsters that they dropped off a couple of hours ago are now stripy (and not in a good way).

5:07 p.m.
Oh noooooooo. Just found one huge orange, black and brown stain on Mrs Griffin's white velvet curtains. Also saw one kid leaving the scene of the crime with a fairly clean mouth. Wonder if these two events could be related?

5:15 p.m.
Gotta run – Ali is cutting me in half. I crunch up in the top half of the box with my head sticking out and Siobhan crunches down in the bottom half with her legs sticking out. I could probably get thrown out of the Magic Circle for revealing so much. Wow. I see Ali has decided to use a real saw. And breathe. Everything. Will. Be. All right.

5:20 p.m.
Have survived being sawn in half. Ali threw strawberry laces out into the crowd as he was sawing like it was our guts. How gross is *that*? The kids were going wild.

6:52 p.m.
Just seen my dad in the street, he must have been on the way to a job. He had a big box of tools and he looked like they were really heavy. I was just about to shout after him when I saw Uncle Conor in his massive stupid car

on his stupid iPhone, which I THINK BY THE WAY he doesn't even know how to use that much. Anyway Uncle Conor was just sitting there watching my dad with this stupid look on his face like he'd beaten him at squash or something. Dad then dropped the toolbox and Uncle Conor just carried on with his call – he didn't go to help or anything. I couldn't get to help Dad then, Uncle Conor would have seen me and I didn't want him to. I began to think though that maybe not everything is OK between them, maybe Dad isn't really happy working for Conor again. I felt really sad to think of my dad being upset. As soon as he gets in tonight I'm going to go downstairs and make him a cup of tea and tell him everything will be all right.

7:07 *p.m.*

At home. Exhausted. Positive I was never as much hard work at my own birthday parties. I have been using some of Mum's v. expensive cleanser and yet my hands are STILL the colour of Eavanne's fake tan. I doubt they will ever go back to their natural colour. I am also aching all over because they all wanted the funky tiger dance and it was worse than being at Killer Kennedy's class. I am rueing (?) the moment I decided to put Amelia's snake in the dance – all that throwing myself on the floor – why didn't I just put a couple of body pops in it instead? Was funny though seeing all the kids throwing themselves on the ground shouting 'Look at my tiger dance' and 'Do it again, Aisling, do it again'. I tell you I am funky tiger-ed out. But, Amelia, my friend – next time I see you, I'm gonna *so* show you how to snake it down!

Wow. Today Parties-to-Go were *amazing*.

7:23 p.m.

As soon as I heard the door go, I went down to see my dad. I said, 'Is everything all right, Dad? With Uncle Conor?' He said straight away 'Why?' and I couldn't say I'd seen him but hadn't helped him so I just shrugged. I gave him a massive hug and told him I loved him. I started to tell him all about my day and how I'd been nearly killed by his and Ali's plan to successfully saw people in half. Dad was really laughing and saying how much he would have liked to have seen my face when I saw the real saw. I was really glad that I was able to make him laugh. He laughed really hard when I said, 'But how am I supposed to be a competition-winning Irish Dancer with no body from the waist down, huh?'

Then I got a text from Siobhan. She said to get online straight away.

7:35 p.m.

Wow – Parties-to-Go are practically the stars of YouTube.

One of the parents must have taken a video on their phone and put it up on YouTube. It's a video of Ali sawing me and Siobhan in half. Underneath it says, 'This is what happened when we didn't pay this company for our children's party. But don't worry, Parties-to-Go, we won't do it again.' Underneath there's loads of comments and loads of people talking about how to get in contact with us for their kids' parties. Wa-hey!! We're in business.

Sunday 5 October

MEL: OMG. So which half am I speaking 2? Top or bottom?

AIS: Ha.

MEL: Sounds like ur having loads of fun without us now.

AIS: No. I really miss u. It's just a stooopid school project.

MEL: So I'm still your BFF?

AIS: BFF. I'm going 2 find out from Mum when I can go 2 Boston this week.

MEL: Yay. How's the boy next door (BND)?

AIS: Cool. BND loves the way I move.

MEL: Lol. Phil was asking about u.

AIS: Wow. I mean who?

MEL: U funny! He didn't ask Colleen in the end :D Gotta run, luv me xx.

7:50 p.m.

So Phil *didn't* ask Colleen to the formal? Oh so what? I'm over him. O.V.E.R. I'm not interested in immature crushes any more.

8:00 p.m.

So, Murphy's Bebo profile has twenty-seven luvs. Guess how many of them are from Eavanne? 19. NINETEEN.

Guess how many luvs he's given to her? 1. ONE. She loses nineteen to one. You lose again, Eavanne.

Monday 6 October

We've had over 300 hits on YouTube. I put my USA National Irish Dance Final dance on YouTube last year and that's only ever had 47 hits and I'm pretty sure most of those were from Dad's computer. We are *famous*. This is what it must feel like to be a celebrity. Some of the first-formers were screaming at me in the corridor and shouting, 'That's the girl who got sawn totally in half'. Ali said people who had never spoken to him before were coming up to him and asking him how you saw people in half. He was saying that – as a member of the Magic Circle – he can never reveal how his magic is done. Ha. He's actually quite funny, if that hadn't been my joke in the first place.

FLASHMOB

Tuesday 7 October

Murphy and his mates were in the IT room today looking at their video site. Apparently it's not going very well. They've only got 609 votes (and 12 of those are from me and the FITZSIMON clan under various aliases). Rory has about four different email accounts. Why? I just don't know. He actually charged me two euros for two votes. Is *nothing* sacred?

Wednesday 8 October

3:37 p.m.

OMG. Kennedy has actually locked me out of dance class. Oooh, I tell you, that woman is a *witch*. A horrible, shouty, mean, pointy-nosed, competition-obsessed, knee-slapping and now door-locking WITCH. I was only *five* minutes late and that was only because I had to find Murphy to tell him I didn't need a ride home. I saw her walking across to the dance room, Murphy actually waved at her, lol, and only got a scowl back.

And now, two minutes later I got to class and she'd locked the door. I gave her my Aisling Hard Stare through the windows of the door but I had to go on tiptoe, which I think made it lose some of its impact. Even so, she didn't so much as *look* in my direction – much too busy shouting and ruining everybody's lives.

3:40 p.m.

I'm gonna miss going through the routines for team selection. And Kennedy needs to decide who to put into the competition team because the preliminaries are just over a week away. Oh yes, the road towards the big old Irish Dance world championship begins. This is *so* typical.

3:56 p.m.

I was telling Ali and Siobhan about KK and I saw them do that raised eyebrows thing about me being late. Apparently I am a little bit late now and then, so I had to promise on my Irish honour not to be late any more.

It's never my fault – I always just seem to be in one place doing one thing when I'm supposed to be in another place doing something different.

These are the changes in my life I'm going to make. All changes to come into effect immediately:

1. Practise for my Irish Dancing and get on to the competition team.
2. Be on time. Have no tolerance for lateness and those who indulge in it.
3. Do not let Killer Kennedy bother me. Rise above it all.
4. Stop taking a walk round the garden to try to see into Murphy's bedroom.

8:00 p.m.

Ali's just left. Him and Rory have been working on this 'HoudinAli' routine in which Rory puts Ali into a straitjacket wrapped in rope and then locks Ali into a shed. Everyone then counts down from fifty to see if he can escape. Rory has been helping him out – Ali wanted Rory to set fire to the shed to 'increase the stakes' but Dad came leaping out into the garden and took the matches off Rory just in case.

Ali's desperate for the chance to show off 'HoudinAli' at a party. We thought after our incredible success of Saturday we'd be booked solid for months. But guess what? Our next kids' party booking is for . . . wait for it . . . *six* weeks' time. What? Apparently all the mums of Dublin start planning their parties up to a year in advance. Are these people *insane*? Have they not ever heard of TGI Friday's? Ali's furious. He stomped off and all the ties from his straitjacket kept bashing into things as he walked through the house. We all sat in silence for a bit and then Rory started laughing and then I started laughing and then Siobhan said I wonder how many issues of *Pulse* will be out before we do our next party, and then I didn't feel so much like laughing again.

10:00 p.m.

I know Murphy isn't home yet. Maybe he *is* a degenerate. What on earth can he be doing until this time of night?

11:00 p.m.

Murphy home – I can turn off my shuffle and go to sleep. This is what it must be like to be the parent of a degenerate teenager.

11:05 p.m.

Quite hard to sleep knowing Murphy is a mere five metres away from me. Perhaps I can borrow Dad's drill from the shed and drill a hole through the wall. I bet I could get away with it. No one ever expects that sort of behaviour from sixteen-year-old girls. If I was a forty-year-old bloke I'd have to go to prison but *I* could probably just grin at the police and say I was just worried about my neighbour getting home because he rides a scooter so I drilled a hole in the wall so I could check. I'd probably get a medal or something for being so caring. Ha ha.

ARGGHH. Just thought, that would mean that he could see me with my mouth open, dribbling while asleep. Yeuch. OMG if I drilled through I'd have to wear mascara all the time even in bed, like my Aunty Jo 'in case there's a fire'. No no no no no. No drill. Forget it.

Why do I even care, it's not like we're even going out. We're just mates. Are we mates? You can't really go out with someone if they're not going out with you, can you? Unless you're Eavanne, that is. Freak alert.

I'm going to go to sleep thinking about Phil Donnelly, maybe I can re-like him instead. Oh, who am I kidding? I can't re-like Phil Donnelly. What's to 're-like'? That's not even a thing. The truth is . . . well, the truth is I like Murphy – and probably more than just as a friend. And in fact now I actually write it down, I realize I want to really get to know him. Oh no. This is going to be complicated. I don't know what he thinks about me. That, my 'friends', is the ten million dollar question.

11:10 p.m.

OK, it's late, but let's look at the evidence. Lists always make things better.

1. He gives me rides on his scooter.
2. He apologized for his friends (welcome friend, Dec, and one knucklehead, JP).
3. He's definitely *not* going out with Eavanne (although she says they are).

Evidence against:

1. He hasn't asked me out or kissed me.
2. He's never spent any time with me that wasn't about the dancing.
3. He still hangs round with Evil Eavanne.

In conclusion I have to conclude that I have absolutely NO IDEA what he thinks of me. That was one of the most pointless lists I have ever written.

Friday 10 October

There has been no further evidence either way in the great Does He or Doesn't He Want to Go Out With Me scientific experiment. I have no further evidence to present, m'lud. I did, however, walk into a big 'discussion' between the parents tonight. It was obvious they were talking about Uncle Conor, because they always are these days and anyway then they stopped as soon as I came in. Mum said, 'Oh we were just talking about . . .' And I said, 'What a big ass Uncle Conor is?' And they both really laughed. Mum told me off for swearing but, as I told her, I could have said a lot worse. I could have said what a 'bum-headed, fat-faced twerpington Stanley Gittings the Third' he is, which wouldn't actually be swearing but would be a lot worse. However, as usual I didn't remember that particular insult that Amelia and I developed for exactly this kind of situation over the summer holidays. I should perhaps have that tattooed up my arm like Angelina Jolie to remind myself. Although by the time I'd had it tattooed I'd probably remember it, like that quote from *Romeo and Juliet* I wrote on my arm for the English test. *Totally* pointless. However, good idea for revising: write everything you need to know all over your body in eyeliner pencil and then you remember it. Hmm – already thinking this is a terrible idea. BYE.

Saturday 11 October

Guess what? The ninth birthday party to end all birthday parties that my cousin Shane was having has been postponed. Guess what number two? PartyKins (our main rival) has double booked. Aunty Stell threatened them with all sorts but because the other booking is for one of U2's little darlings' parties they won't budge. They say Aunty Stella never sent an email to confirm. I wonder if she'll think the obvious: Parties-to-Go!

11:08 a.m.

How obtuse *is* Aunty Stell? She called Mum in a right state saying, 'Shane's birthday is ruined' and 'she'll never be able to find anyone as good at such short notice'. I'm sorry, Aunty Stell, I love you and all but . . . DUH.

When Mum put the phone down, I said maybe they could use Parties-to-Go. But then I felt a bit uncomfortable, like working for the other side. Dad, however, thought it would be great, I think he's really proud of me.

Anyway so Mum said she would call Aunty Stella to see if she wants a bit of the Parties-to-Go Magic. Ha. I made a joke without even realizing it.

9:00 p.m.
Dad's record collection turned up today. Would it be really mean of me to think that I wish that it hadn't?

11:00 p.m.
All right. Enough already. It really *is* the dirgiest music in the world. Would it kill him to play a little bit of Girls Aloud now and then?

Sunday 12 October

I didn't see or hear M all day today. Murphy, where are you? Are you thinking of me?

Hours spent on the Internet looking at Murphy dancing: four.

I think that shows brilliant self-control.

Wednesday 15 October
3:55 p.m.
Just ducked out of Irish Hell Dance for some water. I swear KK was in control of basic training for soldiers in a previous life. She KILLED us today in class. Poor Anya had to do her part in the three-part reel EIGHT times to get it right. She is *so* perfect at the dancing but it's all *so* staid. I wonder if I look like that? Somehow I don't think so – I think I move with the rhythm more. But probably

not, maybe everyone feels like that. Anyway I was sweating so much, KK pursed her lips at me and said, 'Well, maybe if you were here more often you wouldn't find it so challenging'. THAT IS SO UNFAIR, I only missed one class and that's because KK locked me out herself. How on earth can that be *my* fault! I gave her my Aisling Hard Stare – I am getting so fed up of her.

3:59 p.m.

No sign of Murphy, I thought he might be waiting outside for me to see if I was going to the flashmob – but he wasn't – I feel like I haven't seen him for like a hundred years.

4:01 p.m.

Just run into the Wicked Witches (East and West) themselves. They were probably trying to find some newts and bats for their latest spells. There I was in all my Irish Dance kit feeling like such a fool, and Sorcha was just laughing at me. Then Eavanne started teasing me for not being Irish enough, or for trying to be *too* Irish or *something*. Then she said 'to leave Murphy alone', that I wouldn't be 'his type', that he would NEVER see anything in 'somebody like me'. It was horrible. I felt sick in my stomach. I wanted to push her away and never see her again. I really tried to ignore what she said, but it sounded true, as if she knew something. I stopped myself from shouting 'How do you know? What has he said to you?' because even if she told me I wouldn't be able to bear hearing it. I know she's right, it's not as if anything's even happened between us. I mean at least she got to *snog* him, even if it was about a thousand years ago, but at least she's got *that*.

Then as I was walking away feeling so furious I ran into Murphy and everything felt like it was all right again. He asked me if I was going to the flashmob with him. He looked so cute, like he was worried I might say 'no'. Like I was gonna turn him down and go back in to Irish Hell Dancing.

5:00 p.m.

OK, this might not be the wisest decision I've ever made in my life but I have just agreed to go with Murphy to the flashmob. If I just can't get to grips with Irish Dance, why should I keep putting myself through it? At least at the flashmob no one is going to be shouting at me to keep my arms down and telling me I'll never win any competitions.

As soon as I was close to him on the back of the scooter, the wind whipping my hair in my eyes, the green countryside zipping by, I could feel myself getting happier and happier – like I used to all the time back in Boston. It didn't matter that I was Irish or American or too old for Irish Dance or not old enough to go out with someone who had a scooter. I was me again, just for a minute, and it felt great.

6:45 p.m.

Just got back. We danced on the sand, in the water, the spray getting everywhere, flying round us as we put our moves out there. There was no right move, just everyone dancing as they wanted to, dancing to the music – when the wind carried it! We danced to everything, the tune of our talking, of the sea and to JP's boom box, of course. There I was with loads of people knowing hardly anyone, on a beach I'd never been to before, in a country that isn't really mine, everyone sharing the sun going down. I danced next to Murphy and I realized I didn't care about what my mum might say, or about Dad and Uncle Conor, I didn't care about missing Amelia and the Charlestown High girls. I didn't care about Parties-to-Go and I didn't even care if Murphy liked me or not. All I cared about was the dancing and being part of everyone dancing there at that moment. It was like nothing I've ever experienced before. Is that what it feels like to fit in, to know who you are, to be grown up?

6:53 p.m.

Aisling Fitzsimons, will you come back to earth please? Just got two texts from Ali asking me where I was, what I was doing and why I wasn't there after class. I couldn't reply – I don't know why I did it so how can I explain to him something I don't even understand myself?

6:56 p.m.

Loads of films of us dancing at the beach are already on YouTube. Murphy and I are in the background of some of them and one of Murphy's signature moves is on there. I was on the computer in the living room and Mum and Dad kept asking me what I was looking at. I wanted to shout out to Mum and Dad 'Look at me, look at me doing what I want to do' and show them the videos on YouTube, but I couldn't. They wouldn't understand, to them I'm still a little girl who gets excited about ice cream and coming second in some regional Irish Dancing competition. They wouldn't understand what's happening to me, because I don't, really. I feel very sad, like I'm a long way from home.

Saturday 18 October

I found some sand from the beach in my jacket. I could remember what it was like just for a second. Then Rory came flying in on his rollerblades and nicked my iPod recharger shouting, 'what are you looking at sand for, you freak?' Some things are reassuringly the same, it seems.

STEP UP

Monday 20 October

OMG. Rory's been selling PlayStation cheats at school. Ha. No wonder he was able to afford all those Magnum ice creams. I knew you couldn't *really* negotiate a 'deep discount' at the local shop. Can't believe I fell for his 'some of us are born good negotiators. Sir Alan, here I come' rubbish. I would love to see him on *The Apprentice* just to hear 'Surallan' say 'Rory Fitzsimons, I've had just about enough of your rubbish, you're fired.'

Mum is absolutely furious but Granny Nora said she wished she'd known – she'd been stuck on the same mission for six months! Lol. It would not surprise me one bit if that was true. I didn't see what the big deal was, although it must be a bit of a shock for Mum but then she's been shielded, she hasn't had to pay him for any favour needed (like I have) over the years. Well, Mum, here's your son, now maybe you'll see what he is *really* like.

But turns out Mum's worried about everyone on the estate talking about us, not having much cash and having to go back and work in the family business, and that somehow Rory thinks we're so broke he's got to help out with the cash. I didn't realize things were so bad.

Now this makes perfect sense, *this* is why we had to come back to Ireland in the first place. *This* is why Conor is so pleased with himself and his stupid car. And *this* is why Dad's so unhappy. I can't believe all I cared about was getting myself a flight back to Boston. This was no big plan to 'come home', this was because our plan to live in the US stopped working when Dad lost his job. From what I know about it, this is the fundamental problem with plans. IMO, they never work out like you want.

5:05 p.m.

Rory is *totally* grounded. But he's being very nonchalant about it. He keeps clicking his fingers and saying 'it's cool'. Mum kept saying 'it most certainly isn't cool', but he still kept saying it. The boy is educationally subnormal, as I have always suspected.

5:30 p.m.
Oh no. Rory being grounded means a whole lot of time with him in his room playing with his mixer, teaching himself to mix. Mum and Dad have not managed to work out that this is pretty much his dream situation, because they have no idea what a mixer is. Perhaps they think he's sitting in his room thinking of ways he can correct his behaviour and not mixing the same two records over and over again and having the time of his life. Poor Mum and Dad. Sometimes I wonder what it's like to be part of the technologically incompetent generation. Bewildering, I should think.

6:45 p.m.
Aunty Stell just called, she heard from the lady who 'does' her ironing that Parties-to-Go are the hot new thing in Dublin for children's parties. Her lady also 'does' for another woman, whose children were Celtic Tigers for the day courtesy of yours truly, and she said we were – and I quote – 'quite simply the best'. This means Parties-to-Go have the gig. Go, Parties-to-Go. GO!! Texted Siobhan and Ali the good news.

7:00 p.m.
Text back from Siobhan saying let's show them what we can really do. Gulp. One back from Ali saying he would

call me later when he managed to get out of his Tomb of Doom, which I HOPE is another magic trick.

7:02 p.m.
Ali out of his Tomb of Doom with only minor scratches. He says that's the last time *he* buys a trick like that on eBay without emailing the seller first. Wise words, I think.

Thursday 23 October
3:00 p.m.
Despite my best efforts and paying Rory the best part of twenty euros, I only managed to drum up fourteen votes for Murphy's video. He looked really sad. Stupid Fat Playaz got 4,000, and they're nowhere near as good! Rory said there's a way of using this program, which creates emails and votes from them. However, he's set the price beyond what the market (i.e. me) can afford. Besides, there has to be another way to get Murphy to dance with Ace FX, which doesn't involve me emptying my piggy bank to Rory.

3:34 p.m.
Mum really keen that Parties-to-Go throw a fabulous party for Shane. I think she wants to show Stella what this branch of the Fitzsimons family is capable of. Don't worry, Mum. The gauntlet is thrown – I won't let you down. Shane will have a party that he will never forget! Oh yes.

4:09 p.m.

Went round to Siobhan's house. We were drinking blackberry and cucumber smoothies. Mmm. Siobhan makes them herself with the hand blender and crushed ice and they are Yum. We looked very sophisticated at the computer with our drinks in long glasses. In a rare break from our Party Planning, Siobhan was asking me about Murphy, about 'me and Murphy' – like we were boyfriend and girlfriend. I mean, if I thought like Eavanne I'd be telling everyone that we are married by now! But I am sooooo much more mature than that witch.

But it DID make me wonder if there actually is an *us*?

OK, everyone, let's do it. It's time for the List of all Lists . . .

Evidence that Murphy could be my boyfriend:

1. He took ME to the flashmob.
2. He smiles at me a lot.
3. He was teasing me about Ali being my boyfriend.
4. He gives me 'the look' – you know, the one a boyfriend gives a girlfriend.

Looking pretty good so far. But . . .

1. There's been no kiss. If we were going out Irish style, surely there would have been a kiss by now? That is what Siobhan said, and that is the crucial missing piece of evidence.

At least in the US we'd either be dating or we wouldn't. Wait! Wait! Hang on a minute, this is crazy. What am I doing? I'm writing a list to see whether I've got a boyfriend or not. Surely the answer is clear. If you have to put a list together – then you don't have a boyfriend. Note to self: Aisling – Murphy is not your boyfriend. Maybe it's *me* who needs the post-it on the bathroom mirror.

4:15 p.m.

Hmm, what I need is a magazine quiz that can answer the question 'Do You Have a Boyfriend?'.

4:17 p.m.

Have been through every back issue of *Mizz* but no joy. No article. :o. Hey, maybe I should write one, I'd make millions. I can't be the *only* girl in the world who's confused as to whether she's going out with someone or not, can I?

4:20 p.m.

Have decided a) I'm completely insane and b) to stop worrying about Murphy and c) to strap on my dancing shoes and to do some serious dance.

Preliminaries Saturday. Yikes!! Play that funky Irish Dance Music and play it loud.

Saturday 25 October
2:00 p.m.

We-hell. What can I say? There's the good news. Things certainly started off all right. I was in time, and my ringlet hairpiece didn't fall out, despite my most radical moves (more of those later). Umm – that's the end of the good news, and here comes the bad news . . .

Just as Killer Kennedy said. Arms straight down, I did all the moves exactly as she said, exactly as we'd practised. Perfectly in time, the best I've ever danced since we got to Dublin. But then something happened, the music began to really change in my head, as if a different music, something from the flashmob, was playing as well. Then I couldn't really see the others or the judges or remember what I'd practised. It was so weird. I didn't really know what I was doing but I guess I must have been doing a couple of my moves, the moves Amelia and I worked out. They just seemed so right, and to match the reel so well, it was only when the music stopped that I realized I'd been doing something different. One of the judges looked straight at me and then wrote something down with a shake of the head that SOOOO was not good. And then I saw Killer Kennedy coming right at me.

I tried to get away as quick as possible and had almost made it to the changing rooms. But Killer Kennedy appeared in the corridor like the Child Catcher in *Chitty Chitty Bang Bang*. And she was awful. She said I hadn't just let myself down but by dancing the way I had, I'd let down the whole team. I hadn't thought of that. Anya and Mushira were with her and they just looked really disappointed, which was sort of worse than being cross with me. I felt really bad for them like I'd let them down. I would never have done this in Boston to Amelia and Lauren. So why have I changed so much? KK said if I hadn't been dancing with Murphy so much maybe I'd have had the time to practise properly and we would have done well.

Now wait a minute, Mrs Kennedy, Murphy? What has *Murphy* got to do with any of this?

Could this be true? Could he be the reason why I'm always late and I'm failing at Irish Dance? He can't be the bad thing in my life, he's the *good* thing in my life.

I went downstairs and made myself a hot chocolate with real chocolate melted into it and with marshmallows and chocolate chips and the squirty cream. Yum. I didn't even try to limit myself to the amount of times I could squirt the cream, let it melt, eat it and then squirt again. On about my eighth time Mum came into the kitchen and started asking me about the qualifying heats. I didn't know what to say. I could have told her what happened. But what happened? No one knows how lame I am just yet – we have to wait until we get the judges' comments for that. And I can't tell her what Kennedy said about Murphy – she'll hit the roof. So after one more squirt of cream for luck, I just told her it went OK. That's not a lie, I mean sometimes really bad can *be* OK, like having one toe sawn off in a freak accident rather than both legs. Anyway, she looked at me and I thought she was going to ask me what actually happened so I just kept stirring my hot chocolate round and round, watching the foam spin round and hoping she wouldn't say anything else. Then, luckily Dad burst in saying that he'd decided he was going to take up golf.

4:06 p.m.

Up in my room. Number of times I've gone to the window to see if Murphy's scooter is there: 26

Number of times Murphy's scooter has been there: 0

4:32 p.m.

Aisling Fitzsimons's Official and Tested List of Songs that make you feel better to listen to:

- S Club 7 – 'Reach'
- Boys Like Girls – 'The Great Escape'
- Abba – 'Dancing Queen'

4:34 p.m.

Songs that should be removed from the iPod of anyone in the midst of an emotional crisis:

- Sinead O'Connor – 'Nothing Compares 2 U'

5:02 p.m.

Number of times Rory has knocked on my door in the last hour: 12

Therefore number of 'Keep Out – Private – Go Away

– Whatever you want I'm not interested' signs needed for my bedroom door: 1

5:03 p.m.

Alternatively I can stick my headphones into my ears harder and pretend I can't hear Rory knocking at the door because of the music. Ha ha ha. Great plan.

5:04 p.m.

Am now also having to pretend I can't hear Rory trying to correspond with me using Morse code by banging on the pipes. I don't even know Morse code.

5:05 p.m.

Nor see that big sign being slid under my door reading 'What you up to, Sis?' in massive letters cut out of magazines. When? When? When will that boy not be grounded any more? It's like trying to contain a whirlwind in a matchbox.

5:05 p.m.

There I was, in the middle of my second hour of trying to work out where I went wrong this morning. The Lupe Fiasco music probably wasn't exactly re-creating the exact environment of the preliminaries. But I'd had enough Irish reels for one day. When suddenly and unfortunately – as usual – in bursts Rory, suffering he says from 'advanced boredom'. He refused to budge until I showed him a few of my b-boying (or b-girling, ha ha) moves.

Not wanting one of those big fights where I get him out of the room and he tries to get back in the room and we both use the door like a massive shield till one person wins, which have seemed to be an everyday occurrence since he's been grounded, I decided, OK, you've asked for it, and I broke out my latest and some might say most impressive move.

5:07 p.m.
What a surprise! Rory is brilliant at it immediately. I must be a fantastic teacher.

6:35 p.m.
Wow. Rory and I have freestyled our way through the afternoon and evening. In fact, I've got more new moves worked out in one afternoon than Amelia and I put together in months of Saturdays. What a laugh!

Names of New Dance Moves Created by Rory and Aisling Fitzsimons:

1. The Swan Neck à Deux. A variation of the Swan. But including a double shimmy before you hit the floor. Done in a pair, of course!
2. The Tigers Come Down From the Mountain. Inspired by the ancient art of T'ai Chi, it has quite unusual crooked arms that swing you in to a half-turn high kick. Hiiii yaaaahhh.
3. Urban Do-Si-Do. Move round each other in a number of jerky but cool steps. I've never seen anything as

good, not even on MTV. Missy Elliot and her crew would definitely get their freak if they saw it.

Damn we are good. Shame there is nothing cool about dancing with your younger brother and no one can ever know. I would deny it – even if they said I could never have ice cream again.

7:01 p.m.
Dad came in and turned off the music. He said he's had just about all he could stand of 'the rap' as he called it. He also wanted to know what happened to songs with melody? And why did everything have to be about cars and jewellery and hotel lobbies? Amount of idea I have as to what he's talking about: none. Love him anyway, though. I said 'Ahh you're so cute' and gave him a big hug. Just because he doesn't understand ANYTHING about music doesn't mean he isn't a tip-top, A1, Class A Dad.

7:03 p.m.
Phew. Murphy just turned up. He'd brought back fish and chips for everyone at his. Ahh. Not only good-looking but incredibly good-looking and thoughtful towards his family but *also* with excellent taste in junk food. Who doesn't love fish and chips on a weekend? After he'd got off his scooter, he looked up at our upstairs window and I – coincidentally – just *happened* to be standing there. He waved. I waved back. He looked lovely under the light

of the streetlight. He gave me the thumbs up and I gave him the thumbs up with a nod, then he smiled. Then he gestured at his fish and chips and I waved goodbye. I think it was one of the loveliest conversations two people have ever had with no conversation, through a glass window and involving fish and chips.

7:04 p.m.
What a day. If you'd told me when Killer Kennedy was coming at me with her eyelashes on full-on flash setting, and that I'd still be going to bed tonight being happy with the way I dance, I never would have believed you.

Monday 27 October
11:00 a.m.
Panic at the computer in the IT room!
   Fat Playaz: 1,000 hits
   Murphy and Crew: 100 hits

11:01 a.m.
I have to find some way of helping Murphy and his crew. They have until Friday to sort something out to get more hits than Fat Playaz. I am worried, if Murphy doesn't win this competition he's likely to fall into some kind of gloomy mood. A mood which will not encourage him to a) finish (not) going out with Eavanne, and b) start dating me properly (you know – not in a way where I have to make lists to try to work it out).

11:02 a.m.

Oh no no no nooooooooooo. There's some good news: Murphy's deep dark moment of panic is over. But there's also some bad news and this is mainly because Murphy has had this ker-azy idea to organize another flashmob. This time somewhere that would get him noticed. Like at the school. Well, actually in the school library, this Friday at 4:00 p.m. And I have agreed to take part. Well what would *you* do? This is *Murphy*.

GULP.

I just couldn't say no. He was just looking at me, right at me, and I felt all gooey inside like a big melted marshmallow. And you wouldn't expect a big gooey marshmallow to say no to anything, would you? Well – neither could I.

Well, I did say I would do anything!! I'm not the sort of girl who goes back on her word to help someone. Yeah, say that to the Head, Aisling, just before she expels you.

Because, if we get caught – it'll be CURTAINS for me. I'll worry about that later – there's actually no way we *can* get caught. You know why? Because we're going to be wearing *masks*.

Gotta run – if I'm any later for the Shane's Party Meeting – I might as well rename the business Parties-have-Gone. Ha ha.

3:08 p.m.

Siobhan and I have noticed that every time we're with Ali he's always looking at his watch as if he can't wait to get away. She teases *me* that he can't wait to get away from all my stories about Irish Dance, I tease *her* that it's because he really fancies her and he's counting the minutes that he can spend with her. Ha ha. Hey, maybe it's because he thinks we're really *boring* and so can't wait to get away. I hope it's not that.

3:12 p.m.
It's not that! Ali's not really allowed to be out that late or his dad really gets on at him. He sounds really strict. Bet his dad doesn't wish he was a hippy and endlessly revisit and change his Top 5 list of the 'Best Live Shows' he's ever been to like mine does.

3:15 p.m.
Tough call. Shane's party of the year has been moved to this Friday. Apparently there was another party-of-the-year on the Saturday so Shane's had to move. Siobhan mentioned it fairly casually and I tried to be casual as well but inside I was shouting *Noooooooooo*. Because it's now on the same day as the flashmob.

Places I need to be on Friday afternoon at the same time: 2

Numbers of Aisling Louise Fitzsimonses in existence: 1

What am I going to do? I can't let Murphy down – I want to help him so much, and I can't let Siobhan and Ali down – they're my only friends here and they're relying on me for the grade in the project.

It will be OK. It will be OK. I'm going to have to do both. I can definitely do both. It will be OK. I can just about get to both and make everyone happy. Jeez. Thank goodness for that. I can do the Library Flashmob at 4:00 at school and then be at the party for 4:30 at Aunty Stell's house – a little on the late side perhaps – but in time for Monsieur Inflatable Castle – and that will mean everything will be OK.

Here's the plan of military operation for Friday:

11:00 Take all stuff from the Non-Stop Party Shop to Aunty Stell's. Blow up balloons, hang streamers, decorate house.
11:30 Put together party bags to be given to children guests on leaving the party.
12:30 Assemble Ali's crate/box for sawing in half trick.
1:00 Set up face-painting area.
1:15 Dress cake with Disney figures.
2:00 Help Siobhan to get/cue the music for the party games.
2:35 Wrap presents for winners of the games.
3:30 Final checks. Make sure everyone is happy (Aunty Stell, Siobhan, Shane, Ali and me – in that order).
3:37 (at the latest) Leave Aunty Stell's and run over to school.
3:50 Arrive school – get changed. DO NOT FORGET MASK.
4:00 Go to Murphy's flashmob. Be a brilliant dancer and WOW him into deciding I am the one for him.
4:15–4:17 Get changed. Quickly!
4:17–4:29 Run like the wind between school and Aunty

Stell's house. Do not stop to help old ladies across the road, to pet kittens or pull tights up.
4:30 Get to Shane's party. Hand over deposit to inflatable castle man. Get sawed in half. Put in another Ace performance for Parties-to-Go.
6:32 And relax.

Hmm. Is this even *possible*? Have I gone *bananas*?

3:16 p.m.
Wait. Whoa there. Here's an idea, if the mountain won't come to Mohammed? Hey maybe I can get Murphy to change the day of the flashmob, maybe he could do it on Thursday or Saturday instead and then I wouldn't have to challenge the under-18 Irish record for the 800-metre dash. Sometimes I'm so good – I amaze myself. I will call this PLAN B.

3:17 p.m.
Ha. Just had a very scary walk home. I've got the deposit for the bouncy castle in my pocket: two hundred euros. Parties-to-Go are to pay the inflatable man (!) themselves. I had to keep very alert for potential thieves and robbers. But now I'm at home and safe, well, I can't help thinking, what would I do first with all this money, if it was mine? I could take Mum, Dad and Rory out for pizza and ice cream? Or I could go down to Top Shop and shop till I drop? Hmm, I'm beginning to understand the criminal mind.

3:30 p.m.

Or I could pay Rory to get that program that automatically votes for Murphy and his crew to win the competition. Blimey – that is a tempting idea – he'd definitely forget Eavanne then. No, no, no. I have to keep it safe, because it's the deposit for the bouncy castle. Bouncy castles before boyfriends every time! Did I say *boyfriend*?

3:45 p.m.

Amount of times I checked the money to make sure it's still there: just twenty-two! I *knew* I needed that plastic safe that Mum chucked out when we moved here. Still, I've found a biscuit tin and once I had eaten the biscuits, put the money inside and hidden it I felt much better.

3:50 p.m.

This is how those pensioners must feel with all their money in the world put in a tin stuffed under the bed. I doubt I shall be able to sleep tonight. The responsibility is *enormous*. I hope I never become a zillionaire like Richard Branson, I would not be able to cope. I would also need an extremely HIGH bed.

5:09 p.m.

Probably don't need to sit here watching the tin. It will probably be all right if I go downstairs and fix myself a sandwich.

5:11 p.m.

Back again. I wasn't that hungry anyway and besides you can't be too careful. Why did Siobhan think of saying she was hopeless at losing things? So wish *I'd* said that first.

Wednesday 29 October

Sooo, we got our results back from Saturday's competition. And what a horror show they turned out to be. Mrs Kennedy stood in front of the class like some kind of female dictator. I swear she was *pleased* that the results were so bad. Eyelashes were up to number ten on the scale of flashingness.

She kept on and on and on about how SOMEBODY's arms were bent, that SOMEBODY's toes weren't even pointed. Like it was this big drama.

We all knew who SOMEBODY was, oh yes. I had to stop myself from shouting: 'I know you're talking about me, I'm not doing this on purpose – I try the hardest I can to do what you ask me to, I just can't do it. I'm not used to it, I never will be used to it. Please leave me alone'. But I didn't say anything.

It was so unfair on Mushira and Anya. All they did was the best they can do, and Killer Kennedy was making them feel awful about the way *I* danced, as if it was all *their* fault. And then I got to thinking. These horrible thoughts kept unfurling in my brain a bit like a rope that's been coiled up and let loose over the side of a boat. Round and round went the same thoughts as she was flashing away: why should I just keep doing this? I'm letting the other girls down. I don't fit in here. And then I kept repeating over and over the same question in my mind: 'Why am I doing this?', 'Why am I doing this?' And I couldn't think of a single reason *why*. And so I left. I just walked out, left the dance room, left Killer Kennedy and left Irish Dancing. If they don't want *me* then I don't want *them*.

Besides, Irish Dancing is just for kids. I go to flashmobs, I've got a (sort of) boyfriend with a Vespa, I'm not a kid and I don't want to be treated like one, thank you very much.

It feels brilliant that I never have to have KK flaming at me any more, AND I don't have to feel like I've let down the others. So, if anyone cares I feel fine. I'm sure Mum and Dad will understand this when I tell them. I ran all the way home. What a relief. No more Killer Kennedy.

6:30 p.m.
Saw Murphy after dance class. Unfortunately there's no way he can do Saturday because the competition finishes on Friday and he wants to post the flashmob almost live so NO ONE can copy him. Oh well, looks like we're back to Plan A.

Thursday 30 October
NEWS JUST IN: Siobhan says Murphy and his mates nearly got EXPELLED from school last year for doing something at the school. She wouldn't say *what* exactly

and before I could ask her she started talking about me being on time on Friday. This can't be right – surely if they nearly got expelled *last* year, they wouldn't do the same thing *this* year, would they? Actually, I can kind of see JP not having the brains to realize, but Murphy – noooo way, right?

Days gone by without telling my mum about quitting Irish Dance lessons: 1

One is OK – anyone can forgive 'One' day, right? One day is completely forgivable. Umm. This I know. Day One is just the day when you choose the right moment and the right words.

4:12 p.m.
Granny Nora gave me the weirdest look when I got back tonight, like she knew all about Irish Dance class and Murphy and everything. I wanted to tell her everything. But, how could she in her sixties understand that I don't want to do Irish Dancing any more, that I feel happier hanging out with a boy my parents don't like who rides a scooter? I'm not even sure *I* understand what's happening to me, so how on earth could she? But I had to call Murphy so I went to my room and left her chatting to Mum.

Friday 31st October
7:01 a.m.
This is it. It's here. The day of the Library Flashmob and Cousin Shane's party. And breathe.

Last night I dreamt I was stuck underneath a huge inflatable castle, which looked a bit like Killer Kennedy and everyone was bouncing up and down on it, Mum, Dad, Aunty Stell, Eavanne, Siobhan and Ali. Murphy was trying to get me out but every time he tried to grab me I'd slip further underneath. I wonder what *that* means?

I also wonder how it's all going to go.

Well, there's only one way to find out.

Wish me luck!

8:03 a.m.

I believe I'm in the midst of advanced panic. I can't do this, there's no *way* I can do this. The only thing that runs totally on time is Swiss cuckoo clocks. I'm bound to be late for Siobhan and Ali and Shane's party. So instead I'm gonna hide under my duvet all day and pretend I never heard of flashmobbing, Parties-to-Go or even Dublin.

Wait. This is not the good old Aisling Fitzsimons we all know and love. *Of course* I can do this. Arise, Aisling, from your bed, take your hand from that big bag of Doritos and go and conquer the world. Or a kids' party and a school library at least.

😬

10:07 a.m.

We got our masks. They're kinda cool and a bit scary. Like in the Batman movies. Well, it is Halloween after all, and you've gotta celebrate somehow. Although I think this is gonna be the scariest Halloween I've ever had.

10:09 a.m.
Murphy has confirmed kick-off time is 4 p.m. All running as smoothly as a Swiss cuckoo clock so far. Murphy's also said he'll give me a ride over to Aunty Stell's afterwards, therefore reducing my need to run like the wind. I know I'm not technically allowed to go on the back of his scooter but it saves me time and a lot of running. Besides, I look really inelegant when running. It's one of the things I would like to improve but when am I ever going to find the time for that?

3:30 p.m.
Final checks with Siobhan and Aunty Stell at Aunty Stell's house. I think Parties-to-Go has the right mix of organization and pizzazz! Lol. Especially Ali.

3:45 p.m.
Three texts already (two from Siobhan and one from Ali), both gently reminding me not to be late. Yikes. I keep telling myself, everything will be OK as long as we keep to schedule.

3:52 p.m.
Oh No. Dublin . . . we have a problem. The video camera's stopped working. What are we going to do? JP says it's 'just packed up'. But Dad says bad workmen always blame

their tools. IMO, things don't 'just pack up'. And if they do, the worst thing to do is to start taking them apart, which is just what JP seems about to do. Noooooooooo.

3:54 p.m.

Also IMO things that are mendable do not have little wires hanging out of them. Being the daughter of a plumber, this I know. Beginning to get that weird feeling inside where you can't stand still and keep wanting something to happen but it doesn't happen and then you start to feel a bit out of control. You know the feeling. PANIC.

3:55 p.m.

OK, so we're gonna pool resources and get some money together to buy another one, use it for the flashmob and then return it to the store and get the money back. I handed over my twenty euros. It sure was pretty hard to explain the two hundred euros I also had was for a bouncy castle deposit and couldn't be used. Murphy had looked so relieved when he saw the cash in my hand. I wish I could just let them have the bouncy castle money but I can't, can I?

I *know* everyone's thinking all I have to do is hand over the bouncy castle money and everything will be OK. I'm trying to ignore all the pleading looks. Mind you, if I did, we could just get the camera, do the library flashmob, return it and I could just, just, *just* still make the bouncy castle man. Couldn't I? I mean it would be *tight*, but it was tight anyway.

Aisling Louise Fitzsimons, you're surely not going to just hand over Aunty Stell's bouncy castle money to Murphy's crew now, are you? Are you?

3:59 p.m.
Yep! That's exactly what I'm going to do. Well, what choice did I have? How else are they going to get to dance with Ace FX?

No, *I* couldn't think of any other way either.

Here's the revised schedule.

Oh no – there's literally no time to write the schedule, it's time to just get on with it.

4:05 p.m.
Siobhan DID NOT sound happy when I called her to say I was running late. She went really quiet before putting on her really stern voice. She said, 'Whatever's going on, Aisling, do not be late for the bouncy castle. That's all I ask.' That's all she asks? At the moment, that's Everything. I said, 'There's no way I'll miss that. No way in the world.' But as I'm standing outside the library, with a ghoul mask in my hand, waiting for the Chief of the Blockheads (or JP as he's more generally known) to come back having spent the bouncy castle money on a camera, I'm really not sure I will make it back. Why didn't I just prepare her for the possibility I might be late?

From where I'm standing, things are not looking good! I'm going to turn my phone off until after the flashmob. I'm only going to be a tiny little bit late.

4:30 p.m.

Wow. Wow. Wow. Wow. Wow. Un-believable. We *totally* rocked the Library. I was so nervous at first but as soon as I heard the music I had no choice but to moooove to the music. Murphy and I jumped up on the library tables and there were students actually working at the tables, with their books and everything. When we burst through the doors, everyone looked like they'd seen a ghost – well, several ghosts actually thanks to the masks. Eavanne and Sorcha were at the table Murphy and I were dancing on, which was pretty much *perfect*. I was *so* tempted to take off my mask at that point. 'Look who's dancing with Murphy, Eavanne?' But the thought of being expelled put me off. All I wanted was just to be part of something cool and it was.

Then just as soon as we'd started we disappeared again. Out the fire doors, down the fire exit and we were *gone*.

What a feeling!

And now we're just getting the camera sorted so we can take it back. I'm a tiny little bit on the late side, but nothing turning up with the deposit can't smooth over. Dec's going to package it up good as new . . . so we can . . . Oh no, oh no. Not that. *Anything* but that . . .

4:32 p.m.

It's broken! The camera, the one I bought with the bouncy castle money is broken. I keep looking at it as if it's going to magically come together again like it broke apart but of course I know it won't. And I'm starting to get that really sick feeling inside that things are about to get much, much worse.

JP was handing the camera to Dec and it slipped out of his hands on to the floor and *smashed*. And with it any hopes of us getting the deposit money back now. How am I going to find two hundred euros?

And even worse the two Wicked Witches followed us out of the library on to the fire escape. I think they took some pictures with their mobiles. How can things have gone so wrong?

4:55 p.m.
Well. That's that.

Edited highlights include:

1. Siobhan offering the bouncy castle man her Xtra Vision card as collateral followed by Bouncy Castle Man getting back in his van and driving away.
2. Aunty Stell going all red in the face and sacking Parties-to-Go.
3. Siobhan getting stuck and having to wriggle out in front of the whole party after the sawing-in-half trick didn't work.
4. Me running after Siobhan and Ali while they practically refused to say anything to me.
5. Ali's dad finding out our project was not at the hospital like he thought it was. I thought he was gonna burst a blood vessel when he saw Ali in his moustache and red satin cape.

I guess you could say the magic of Parties-to-Go is over. What's for sure is my friendship with Ali and Siobhan is definitely over.

Murphy won his competition. He gets to dance with Ace FX. At least somebody's happy. I guess. I feel pretty weird about that though, like an Easter egg with nothing inside.

5:23 p.m.
GULP. What are Mum and Aunty Stell going to say?

How did I make such a terrible mess of things? I wish I could go back and change things. Not hand over the money or stop Dec from dropping the camera or arrive at the party to help Siobhan and Ali and not walk out of Irish Dance class, not do *any* of it, and then maybe things would be OK.

7:00 p.m.
I've been lying on my bed trying to work out how everything went wrong, but I can't – everything's so confused, and I can't talk to anyone.

Monday 3 November
So we failed our Transition Project. Even though Miss O'Connor said she knew there were complications, we all still failed. I feel really sick about this. But not as sick as Ali and Siobhan do, I guess.

11:09 a.m.

The school witches turned in the pictures of us at the library to the Principal. Of course they can tell it's me and they're making me tell them who the others are. They tricked me into saying that we all went to school together, but I think that's all I told them. The Librarian was really horrible to me and kept saying she knew I knew who they were. Chillax, Librarian! It's not like we burnt all your books. All we did was try to introduce a little life into the Library. In the end I took all the blame, I didn't rat out Murphy or any of his crew. As if. When I came out of the Principal's office Murphy and everyone were just sitting there waiting to go in.

12:30 p.m.

We've all got detention together. Boooooring. Oh well, at least we're all in it together. What is it they say? Small consolation? I wonder how the Principal found out it was them?

3:45 p.m.

So we've got Ratface Hughes for detention. I would be fairly surprised if he could see us doing anything without his glasses. It wasn't too bad as detentions go, at least I got to look at Murphy for some of it. I kept smiling at him, but he was really cool with me though. He just looked straight ahead. What's wrong with him? What have I done?

3:56 p.m.

Can't catch Murphy's eye at all. What's going on with him?

3:58 p.m.

Bingo. I've worked it out. I saw JP say something to Murphy about me, and Murphy looked straight at me, really coldly, and nodded, like he was really agreeing with JP. Murphy thinks I ratted him out! He thinks *I'm* the one who told on him and the others. How can he *think* that? After all I've *done* for him. After getting Rory to get him all those votes, after giving up Irish Dance so I could dance with him, after ruining my Transition Project, and losing pretty much every friend I've made since we moved here, just so he can get to dance with Ace FX. After all that he still thinks I would just tell on him. I can't believe it. I'm sitting here in detention, looking straight at him, my heart is pounding and I just want to scream at him: Murphy, you clown, don't you know how I feel about you, don't you know I would do/have done pretty much anything I could to help you out and you won't even *look* at me. Well forget it. I can't do any more.

5:56 p.m.

Just walked straight home after detention. I didn't want to even see Murphy. And I definitely didn't want to hear him start talking about how I ratted him out. No way.

I was so pleased to see Granny Nora at our house. I gave her a massive hug, which almost put her off her

GTA. I'm beginning to worry that she is actually addicted to the game. Why Rory should have introduced a sixty-something woman to *Grand Theft Auto* I'll never know. I have noticed he's not so keen to play her now since she's started beating him.

As soon as I released her from the big hug she crashed the car on purpose. She must have really wanted to talk to me, because she really *hates* to crash. She kept asking about dance practice, it was really hard to answer because it doesn't really matter to me any more. I kept getting the feeling that she wanted to talk about something else, you know, how adults sometimes get when they won't say what's on their mind.

She said Aunty Stell isn't going to tell Mum about the party, or non-party, more like. Granny Nora says it's OK sometimes to have secrets. But then she also said it's never OK to not be honest with yourself. Which has been making me think, have I been honest with myself?

6:15 p.m.

Ice cream is the answer. I was in the kitchen trying to make myself the biggest, most comforting banana split sundae the world has ever seen. Which is as follows. Three bananas. Three slices of Neapolitan ice cream. Toffee sauce. Fudge sprinkles (we didn't have any but I cut up some of Mum's fudge into really tiny, tiny pieces and sprinkled those on top). Squirty cream (as much as you can get away with without actually finishing the can, so Mum can't tell you off). More chopped bananas. For the particularly health conscious a big handful of chopped-up nuts. Finish off with melted chocolate sauce. And prepare to say Yu-hum.

It was quite hard to find somewhere to eat the mammoth 'Aisling Goes Bananas' Sundae what with Granny Nora on the PS in the sitting room, Rory doing his 'day trading' from the stairs (don't ask – I have no idea) and Mum doing the ironing on the landing upstairs. Then I had a genius idea. The shed in the garden – at least there I can get peace and quiet. Surely, I thought, no one can be in the garden. I went into the garden and was halted by the wall of sound that was a humdinger of a ding-dong going on in the garden. In the red corner: Uncle Conor, and in the blue corner: Dad.

I guess they'd gone out there so they couldn't be heard. Mistake number one, Dad and Uncle Conor. At *that* volume you could probably be heard by half of Dublin.

Conor was saying Dad can't just come to Dublin and expect to be accepted by everyone. Yes, Uncle Conor, I SO know that that's not the case. I think everyone in Ireland's certainly made that clear to the returning branch of the Fitzsimons family. I heard my dad saying it was his work that got the company going in the first place and now he's getting no thanks for it. I think Dad means having to work like one of the lads. I think I really understand where Dad's coming from. Nothing's worked out like I thought it would since we moved to Dublin. All I've tried to do is the right thing for everyone and I've ended up pleasing no one. Something's gotta change, but what?

MAKING UP

Tuesday 4 November

OK, that's enough of feeling sorry for myself, and trying to hide away in ice-cream sundaes. All right, everybody, I messed up with the Transition Project and I need to apologize to Ali and Siobhan. But it's not like I deliberately set fire to the school or started torturing Bengal kittens, I can make this right. It's time for the official launch of Operation Make Amends. And I already have a genius idea for what to buy Siobhan to make up.

Operation Make Amends. Day 1.

The Apology.

8:44 a.m.

Had to run down the street like mad to catch up with Ali and Siobhan, just so I could apologize to them. How undignified is *that*? I can only hope that the overall standard of my apology was not affected by my sweaty face and out-of-breathness. I apologized as soon as I caught up, but they wouldn't accept it. Siobhan shouted at me, said I'd lied to her and let her down and embarrassed her. Ali walked away with her and they didn't look back. Guess who did see them walking away from me. Only Eavanne and Sorcha. Of all the people in the world, why did *they* have to be there? Argghhhhh.

9:01 a.m.

Wrote Ali a text. I wrote it out here first to make sure it was OK: *Ali. If only I could do magic as well as you, I'd make what happened on Friday disappear, and pull a Grade 'A' out of the hat for you. Ais xx.*

Perfect.

9:02 a.m.

Sent text to Ali.

9:03 a.m.

Wrote Siobhan a text: *S. I'm sorry I lied about where I was. I thought I had time 2 do both, I thought I could pls every1 but I ended up pleasing nobody. I know this isn't how u would do things, and that's why u don't get in such a mess. Pls b my friend. Ais.*

But I couldn't send that one. It was too long and I know she's going to be too angry to read it properly. What am I going to do? I *really* miss her as a friend. She's kind of quirky and different but I've got used to her ways and I guess I'd started to think of her as a good friend.

6:30 p.m.

Operation Make Amends.

Aunty Stell.

Well, that was all just a little bit too close for comfort. Stell and Conor were slumming it round ours for dinner tonight. Aunty Stell kept asking me these really pointed questions, all about the party business. I tried not to say anything but she kept on. I was sure Mum was going to crack on. And she was asking about the deposit money. I haven't even heard from Murphy. There's just no one to talk to about all this. Gotta run, got to help Granny Nora clean up.

7:03 p.m.

Granny Nora says I should be out having fun and being young. Fun? Young? Oh yeah? Because it sure doesn't *feel* like it. I feel about a hundred and twenty years old and that fun is very unlikely to happen to me ever again. Maybe I should start looking around on the Internet for that dancing nunnery.

7:45 p.m.

I've been looking at all the pictures online of all the championships I took part in back in Boston. I look so different in my green velvet dress – I loved that dress. I look all shiny and happy. No surprise there, that's because I didn't know that my whole life was about to go totally mental.

Wednesday 5 November
12:30 p.m.

As days go, this has to be pretty much one of the worst days ever. No one is speaking to me at school. It's like the first day again, only this time there's no chance of making new friends. I had to eat my cheese sandwiches on my own like a loser. Everyone was laughing and sharing crisps and sitting in little groups. The geeks by the computer block, the plastics near the heaters, the witches hanging round Murphy's crew – what a surprise – and then me, all alone. Again.

Talking of Murphy, he called me about a million times. But I have nothing to say to him. Nothing *good* anyway so it's better to just ignore him. If I'd never met him I'd still be doing OK at school, I'd still have some friends who were talking to me and I'd never have walked out of Irish Dancing.

Another call from Murphy. Why won't he just leave me alone?

Another one. This is getting ker-azy. I did what he wanted, I doubt he ever liked me at all, just needed a girl who could dance for his crew. I lost all my friends and he got his dance with Ace FX, what on earth does he need me for now? Nothing, so why won't he just leave me *alone*?

3:30 p.m.
I saw the other girls going in to Irish Dance. I felt really weird about it. Like a magnet being pulled towards them. I couldn't stop looking at them and trying to listen to what they were saying. They were all chattering about competitions like I used to with Amelia and Colleen and Lauren back home.

3:45 p.m.
Murphy and I had a big row. I told him how he dragged me away from the thing I really loved. He thought I meant

dancing with him. How arrogant to think that. I mean Irish Dancing. I'm still really annoyed with him. I told him I don't know how he could think I ratted him out. He says he knows now it was Eavanne and Sorcha but that's not the point.

3:55 p.m.

He says he's got something to show me. He says if I really want to do Irish Dance then he wants to show me some *real* Irish Dance, not the stuff that Killer Kennedy teaches us. This guy certainly doesn't know how to give in gracefully. I do hope it's not a flashmob round Aunty Stell's house because I am *not* in the mood.

6:40 p.m.

Murphy took me up to the Wicklow mountains on his Vespa. He took me to this tiny pub where all these guys were dancing. But they weren't dancing the staid and boring dance that Mrs Kennedy teaches, they were whooping and hollering and dancing. It was wild. I can't believe that all the Irish Dancing I've ever done is based on these guys. Why can't *we* learn Irish Dancing like that? Why does it have to be ringlets and glitter and competition steps to please the judges who wouldn't know good dancing if it danced all over their heads?

Murphy and I went right into the middle of the dancers. We couldn't really do it but everyone was bouncing around like some kind of mosh pit. If one of the old guys had started crowd surfing I wouldn't have been all that surprised! Lol. Murphy and I kept getting pushed up against each other, at one point I thought he was going to kiss me but maybe it was all the excitement getting us carried away – besides I was too busy watching the old guys do their thing. I would never be able to do a quarter of the moves that those guys can do and some of them must have been in their eighties. Woop woop.

I never knew Irish Dance could be so cool, when I was dancing I felt so free. Free as a bird! Free as a free bird!!

11:15 p.m.
And it was all going so well.

Thursday 6 November

Things I wish my parents hadn't found out all on their own. Volume 1:

1. I lied about being over at Siobhan's watching a video when I was out with Murphy on his scooter.
2. I'd dropped out of Killer Kennedy's Irish Dance class and not told anyone.
3. I'm in detention for trespassing after dancing on a library table.
4. I totally ruined Shane's birthday party.
5. I owe Stella the two hundred euros she gave us for the deposit.

So guess this kind of means that mine and Mum's arrangement (the one in which I tried really hard at school and with Irish Dance classes) is off. I guess this also means that I'm not going home to Boston any time soon. I feel about as low as you can go. In fact it's pretty hard not to find a reason to cry my eyes out over this. Except that none of this is anyone's fault except my own.

3:00 p.m.
Unless . . .

3:15 p.m.
Thanks to being boinked on the head by everything falling off my pin board, I found a leaflet that Kennedy gave me way back when. Because guess what was on the back of that? Only details of the World Championships that are going to be held in the USA. All I have to do is dance my way back into Kennedy's team and into a place in the World Championships and I don't *need* anyone to buy me a ticket to the USA. I can get there all on my own.

So I now have a revised plan for getting things back on track. I am calling this one Operation U S of A. And it goes a bit like this . . .

1. By hook or by crook get back into Killer Kennedy's class.
2. Do whatever it takes to learn the moves the way the judges like 'em.
3. Win a place in the Irish team going to the World Championships in the USA.
4. Go back to the USA, get back my love of Irish Dance,

make Mum and Dad proud again. Be back to good old Aisling Louise Fitzsimons. Hooray.

I have stuck the leaflet back on my pin board BUT the other way round as a daily reminder of where I'm going.

And to those who say it can't be done . . . just watch me.

Sooooooo, getting back into Kennedy's class. Oh, how I wish I had Ali's magic wand. I would stand on the stage, wave my cape and say . . .

And for my next trick I need: an empty classroom, one CD of Irish music (not Michael Bublé), one box of the boom variety and one pair of arms that stay by my side and don't start going all like that character from the Mr Men books with the really long, really wobbly arms – oh yes, Mr Tickle – arms that don't go like him at the first sign of a bit of music with a beat.

But instead I'm going to practise every day in every spare moment until I'm so good Kennedy would be mad not to take me back.

In order to do this I, Aisling Fitzsimons, promise to go to bed early, to eat nothing but healthy food like yoghurt and apples like an Olympic gymnast, to practise every day until I can dance the proper traditional Irish way and to have no distractions. No ice cream, no Bebo, no breakdancing, no hip-hop music. No messing around with Rory. And no Murphy. No Murphy? *No Murphy*.

Them's the rules. I'll tell Murphy tomorrow.

Friday 7 November
(Operation U S of A. Day 1)

Sooo tired. Number of hours spent practising Irish Dance today: 5. The only reason I stopped at home was because Rory came in saying that I was 'giving him one of his heads'. That boy! I know it's because I won't let him join in. I can't – the time for messing around with the rules of Irish Dance are *over*.

Monday 10 November (Day 4)
3:50 p.m.

This is going to be more difficult than I imagined. No matter how much I try, I just can't make sense of some of the moves.

5:10 p.m.

Decided to email Murphy today to ask him to leave me alone for a bit. When really I don't want him to leave me alone at all. But with him involved and the way he feels about Irish Dancing, he's too distracting. Operation U S of A needs all my best attention, and even then there's no guarantee it's gonna work. I have to give it everything.

Wednesday 12 November (Day 6)

Bingo. Thank heavens for Anya. Apparently she'd seen me dancing alone in the classroom struggling with the first few moves of a step yesterday. So today she got behind me so I could see how she did it in the mirror and with her help I had it. Then I messed it up again, but for a moment, I had it!!! And that is the most important bit, by far.

In fact it almost made up for the fact that Siobhan and Ali are still ignoring me. I mean I know I really messed up but *still*? I don't know but maybe it's time they got over it? They can't still be really, really angry, can they? Did I *really* mess up *so* bad?

Murphy called tonight. I watched his name flash on my phone and I felt really sick. I really wanted to answer it, but I must be strong otherwise I'll never get home.

Monday 17 November (Day 11)
Nothing much today. School and practice. Just like it's gonna be tomorrow and Wednesday and Thursday and . . .

Wednesday 19 November (Day 13)
I saw Murphy today after school – just for a minute as I was walking over to the dance room. It was the best minute of my day. Better than ice cream, and that's *saying* something.

Thursday 20 November (Day 14)
A couple of the other girls from class came and joined in with me and Anya when we were going through some steps today. Poor Kerry-Ann couldn't join in because she's fractured her ankle. YIKES. I guess it would be pretty difficult to do the Sean Nós with a fractured ankle.

It felt really great to be dancing as a group of girls again. At one point I caught a glimpse of how we looked in the mirror and we looked . . . well we looked . . . we looked like winners.

If we're allowed to dance together, we CAN win this, I just know it. And we won't need Ali's magic wand to do it.

So let's step it up! It's time for Kennedy to see what I've been up to while her back was turned. Because while she's been home sharpening her tongue and practising shouting I've been dancing my batters off.

7:00 p.m.
Just found myself hanging out at the top of the stairs just by the landing window at the time that Murphy normally gets home. *Bad* Aisling. This is not on message. I see I must be on my guard at all times against slipping back into bad habits. I even found myself suspiciously near to the freezer as well. No ice cream till we ace the competition.

Monday 24 November (Day 18)
All the practice is really starting to pay off. Loads of the girls were there to watch today and they were all really enjoying it. It was a proper craic (lol). I didn't even notice when Killer Kennedy joined the crowd, although Anya said her jaw dropped right to the floor like a cartoon character (DOING!) when she saw who it was everyone was crowding round. I just kept on dancing and then I looked up and there she was, just staring at me. Turns out Kerry-Ann's broken ankle means there's one spare

place to dance in the competitions. Mrs Kennedy says if I make practice every day (on time!) and make sure I do everything by her rules then the place could be mine.

7:00 p.m.

Whatever Rory has written on his white wall on his Bebo page, I did not 'nobble' Kerry-Ann in order to get my place in the dance competition, and I am not like that Canadian ice-skater who had her main competitor's legs taken out before the Winter Olympics. The imagination that boy's got – honestly. Although he's animated this cat so it does all these break moves on his page – it's pretty cool. Enough, Aisling – back to practising the moves in the mirror. Leave the animated cat alone, check your email and get off the computer. Back to practising your moves in front of the mirror.

7:10 p.m.

So, I checked my email and I had an email from Murphy:

To: Aisling Fitzsimons
From: Murphy
Re: Me and You, You and Me

Ais, I know you need space, but it's hard, I really miss you. I never got to tell you that when we were dancing with Ace FX all he was interested in was you. You were every bit of the reason we won that competition and why Ace FX wanted to dance with us. The crew's not the same without you, and neither am I. Murph x.

He walked past the dance room today. I saw him ages before he saw me, but when he looked at me I pretended I hadn't seen him. This is the hardest bit of it all. Much harder than winning Kennedy over or learning the steps. Much, *much* harder.

Friday 28 November

Phase 1 complete. I have secured my place in Killer Kennedy's Irish Dance Team, which is going to compete for the places in the World Championships. One step closer to getting home. I expected Mum and Dad to be really pleased, but they barely noticed. I swear I could have said: 'I saw a kitten on the way home from school', or 'I'm not sure I really like McFly any more' for all the interest they showed. The only time I saw Dad smile was when he realized there were loads more roast potatoes so he could have second helpings. What's a girl to do? Oh well, just three more hours' practice before bed. One thing's for sure, whatever happens at the Championships *no one* will have practised as much as me. A fact I find very comforting.

6:45 p.m.

Rory is being so annoying. Most people would get the message that I don't want to talk about all that break-dancing, but not him. He went on and on and on and on about it. 'Why have you given it up?', 'Why are you doing Irish Dancing again?', 'I thought you were a b-girl, sis'. *So* many questions that boy has. Lorks only knows what he was like when he was two and going through that stage where you ask loads of questions. I'm surprised Mum and Dad didn't give him up for adoption. But then who'd have him? Ahh, only joking, I'm sure there must be worse younger brothers.

He's back again. I turn round to get my hair out of my eyes, and there he is, a non-stop question machine. You know his mobile never stops. How on earth did he manage to get a mobile? I didn't even have one until I was fourteen and here he is with one of those touch-sensitive phones – day trading must be paying well, I guess. He's got this Lupe Fiasco ring tone, which he's remixed himself on GarageBand. Even though he's my little brother, I have to say it sounds pretty cool. Hard not to start shaking yourself down when it goes off, which is fine at home but could be pretty embarrassing at Tesco's.

At one point when his phone went we were both dancing to the tone – I was doing my Irish Dance and he was doing his version of break-dancing or 'watch out you're gonna break something' dancing as I think of it. It was just like we used to do, mixing up all the styles. Rory says tonight we developed a whole new way of dancing; i-breaks, he's calling it – I for Irish, breaks for well . . . breaks. Either way it felt good to develop a whole new dancing style from my bedroom.

Monday / December

I ran into Murphy today. I'd taken a break from practising Irish Dance and found myself practising i-breaks – Rory can get to me even when he's not around, it seems. I got quite into it, ended up grabbing a broom and throwing in a few moves I saw the old guys do when Murphy and I went out to the Wicklow mountains. There I was just dancing round with a broom, round and round and then Boom. Straight into Murphy. I felt really bad, I hadn't replied to his email, I didn't know what to say to him. He made it really easy for me. He said he'd been watching me dance, and the moves he'd seen me do were actually pretty good. So, I showed him a couple of the moves Rory and I worked out. They did seem like they really worked. Shame no one's ever going to see them. I did apologize for avoiding him and he was really cool about it. He was a bit funny about the Irish Dance competition, said he'd been thinking about whether it's more important to win or figure things out for yourself. He gave me that Murphy look again like the time he got cross with me for choosing the Irish Dance over the b-boying. I wanted to say I have figured things out for myself. I have to learn the steps the proper way otherwise I can't win the competition and I know that's the right thing to do. But by the time I'd thought of anything to say he'd gone. How does he always manage to make me feel so unsure just when I think I've got everything well and truly figured out? How?

Thursday 4 December

Great news. Miss O'Connor worked out that Eavanne and Sorcha were cheating at their transition class. With two groups already failed, we might get another go. A second chance to not let Siobhan and Ali down, AND a chance to get a better grade.

11:00 a.m.
Just bumped into Murphy in the corridor in between class. He looked so good but we kind of had nothing to say to each other. I guess I've got my Irish Dancing and he's got his break-dancing and that's that. We don't actually have anything to talk about. It was fine when we had the flash-mobbing to talk about but that's all over now. I felt a bit sad. Well, what did I expect, that he would keep on trying to get in contact with me even though I was totally ignoring him?

5:45 p.m.
I know I should be thinking about the World Championships. But I cannot stop thinking about Murphy. I keep thinking about the way we danced when we went to the beach, how it felt to be on the back of his scooter, the way he smiles sort of more with his top lip than his bottom lip, kind of goofy, kind of cute, cute, cute.

Friday 5 December

Granny Nora just told me the strangest story. We were talking about this woman she knew who was married to her husband who was a plumber, but he got ill and so couldn't work. This woman had to go out to work to support them both, and she decided the way she was going to do that was to become a plumber so she could keep his business going while he was ill. So she went off and enrolled in a class. But the men in the class wouldn't accept her. They would send her off looking for left-handed saws and glass hammers! Neither of which exist apparently, although thinking about it how useful would a glass hammer be? It would just break, instantly. No wonder this woman couldn't find one – no one would set up a company making glass hammers unless they were criminally insane.

Some of the men were really mean and would make sure she got all the really dirty jobs. She would end most days covered in dirt and all messy. Sometimes they wouldn't help her at all. Granny Nora said they did everything to stop this woman doing what she wanted to do. But she didn't stop, she kept at it and learnt her trade. When her husband got better she kept on working with him, making the family business bigger and better for everyone. Granny said she just smiled when people said plumbing was a man's profession – because she knew better.

But the strangest thing about this story is how it ended. There I was thinking about this woman underneath some U-bend somewhere in Dublin fifty years ago, and Granny Nora got this strange glint in her eye. Because SHE was that woman. Granny Nora is the one who enrolled in a plumbing course and got to grips with Victorian heating systems and rainwater tanks. And Fitzsimons Plumbing is the company she set up. Wow. All of us, Conor, Stell,

Dad, Mum, Shane, Rory, Me, all kept in Doritos and Mercedes Benz just because Granny Nora believed in herself and wouldn't let herself be put off by all the people who said she couldn't do it.

Saturday 6 December

Here we go. Competition day. Only the qualifier but still. That news from Granny Nora has rocked my socks off. Makes a flashmob in a library seem like small fry. Blimey, I'd far rather take on Killer Kennedy than a legion of Dublin plumbers from fifty years ago.

But whatever Granny Nora did or didn't do, I must keep my eyes on the main prize. Going to the World Championships.

11:00 a.m.

I am *so* ready for the competition. I check in the mirror just to make sure that I have the right balance of Glitter. Hairpins. Ringlets. Lace. Velvet. And Sequins. I must have seen myself in this outfit 200 times, but today I think I look different. Why? I kept looking at myself for ages in the mirror to see what's different but nothing is new, nothing has actually changed – everything is exactly the same. Do I look strange, or do I *feel* strange?

12:00 High Noon

I'm backstage. If I peek round the corner, I can see Granny Nora, Mum, Dad and Rory are in the crowd.

Here's the math: there are three places for three of us

dancers to go to Irish final and sixty of us competing for them. I may not be the best in the world at math, but that gives me a five per cent chance.

Anya's up first. Good luck, Anya – she won't need it. They might as well give her a plane ticket right now.

12:15 p.m.

Anya danced perfectly. Like a little Irish Dance doll in one of those plastic tubes. Way to go, Anya.

12:30 p.m.

Marie Glennon (aka Contestant No. Two) did not look happy with the way she danced. She left the stage in tears. Oh no. It can happen – you just miss your step and take a little tumble, but you've just got to keep going. Look the judges straight in the eye and keep on dancing. It can really knock your confidence. I've *so* been there.

12:45 p.m.

OMG the next one dances like I used to, the way that used to drive Kennedy nuts. All arms flailing around. The judges looked all snarly as if she was wearing a T-shirt saying 'Irish Dance sucks'. Although it pains me to say it, I've gotta give it to Kennedy. The old Mr Tickle approach to Irish Dancing doesn't seem to be popular with the judges.

And the next contestant is, well the next contestant is . . . well, it's me! Dancer number twenty-seven, will you come in please.

1:00 p.m.

I did it. I think I did OK. All the moves were OK. They must have been OK because KK said 'very well done'. That's actually equal to an Oscar in the real world in terms of recognition. Siobhan and Ali were there and weren't throwing rotten tomatoes in my direction, so that's something, maybe things are on the mend there. You know who else was there? Murphy. I only saw him for a moment, he seemed fed up to see me dance. He just doesn't understand if I had my way I wouldn't dance like that. I don't *want* to dance this way, but it's the only way I can get home, the only way I can make everything right for everyone. That's all.

Gotta run, they're announcing who's going through. Fingers crossed. Toes crossed. Arms crossed. Everything crossed. I need that place.

First place gone to Marie Donovan. Well done, Marie (she said gracefully, while secretly wishing they'd said *her* name).

Second place gone to Anya Kudyba. Well, of course, Anya – she danced perfectly.

And then the third and final place. I feel sick. He's taking so long to announce the name. Find the piece of paper, get your glasses on, and announce the name – how can it possibly take *this* long? This must be how everyone must feel on *American Idol* waiting for them to announce the name of the next person to be evicted. Why such a long gap? I catch Mum's eye – she looks more worried than I do. I wish Rory would take his iPod headphones out of his ears and actually share the moment with his sister. Would that be *too* much to ask?

Wait. Did I just hear MY name? Did they say Aisling Fitzsimons? I thought I heard my name called out. What was that other chick's name, the one after me, it was something really similar, Aileen Fitzpatrick? Maybe they read *her* name. Why is Mum pulling Rory's headphones out of his ears and looking so pleased? Why is he jumping on his chair and clapping? Could it be? Is it . . . is it because I'm through? IT IS. I'm *through*, they said Aisling Fitzsimons. Hey, I'm through to the *final*. One step closer to the USA. Woop woop.

1:45 p.m.
Lead me to ice cream. There's gonna be an ice-cream celebration.

Sunday 7 December
7:30 a.m.
So here it is, the day in which I could qualify for the World Championships in the USA and get that all-important plane ticket home. Excuse me while I go: arrrrrggggghhhhhhhh.

8:00 a.m.
Why is it these days every time I put on all my kit and look in the mirror, I think I look like a chump? It's the same dress, the same make-up, the same glitter that it's

always been. But when I look in the mirror I don't look the same. What's changed, will somebody please tell me?

I keep thinking about that day Murphy and me went up into the mountains, only every time I remember I don't see me on the back of the scooter I see Eavanne. I wish I could stop thinking about it. It makes my stomach feel like scrambled eggs, all mixed up in a pan.

It's probably just nerves from the competition.

10:10 a.m.

Rory's been practising his break moves. He's got it going on. Oh I wish I wasn't dressed like this, I wish I was going to some dance competition where I could really dance the way I want to. I wish, I wish, I wish.

I keep thinking about those dancers, those men in the pub in the mountains. Being in among them, dancing around and trying to copy their steps. When they were my age did they ever try to please everyone by doing the proper steps to the proper music to please some judges? Did they wear costumes and try to get top marks or did they just grab the nearest thing to them, get some instruments together and just dance? What I mean is, they who invented it all, did they do all that so some schoolgirl could wear an inch thick of glitter and prance around in front of some tired old judges? Something's wrong with this picture.

I've got my moves, my routine couldn't *be* more practised. All the family are together and are coming to watch me dance. And as if that wasn't good enough, Granny

Nora has made Dad a director in the plumbing business. Things just couldn't be better for everyone. I can't mess with this right now – I have to do this *right* and show that I *can do* this.

Why, then, when finally everything's going so well, do I feel so sick? You'd think I was being driven to have my tonsils out rather than to dance my way into the World Championships. Well, no time to think about the whys and wherefores now. Gotta get into the car and wow everyone. Wish me luck. Boston, Here I Come.

11:00 *a.m.*
Can you believe it? I'm not sure I can. For just one moment Killer Kennedy was able to talk in a normal voice about something that didn't include keeping your arms in, or keeping your back straight. She actually told us to dance from the heart. She said that's because that's where we keep our Irish tradition. For one moment I actually believed she had a heart and felt all warm towards her. She does really seem to want us all to do well. I don't think it's all about winning the competitions, I think it's about us all doing our best, our very best for ourselves. When I think about it, is that really so bad?

Thing is: I'm not dancing from my heart – at all. I don't know where I'm dancing from, but it's definitely not the heart. When I touch my heart where Kennedy did, I end up thinking about Murphy. You know, I keep thinking, it wasn't his fault that things went so bad for me. Pretty much everything that happened to me was down to what *I* did. Murphy didn't make me lie to Mum, or make me mess up with Siobhan and Ali. All he wanted was for me to dance as best I could and he brought me into his world enough to do that. I was so concerned with finding new friends and fitting in, I didn't even notice that he'd been a friend all along. And you know what? In the end I don't think I really treated him like you should treat a friend. I guess I'll never get the chance to tell him that.

12:10 p.m.

An hour to go and I feel really weird. My feet are virtually uncontrollable. I'm sure my hairpiece isn't on straight and one of the pins keeps pricking me in my neck when I turn my head round quickly. Yes, I know the answer: well, don't turn your head round quickly! But that's the least of my worries, my bodice feels tight, my socks are really itchy and my shoes are really pinching my little toe. I'm so uncomfortable and it doesn't help that I'm sitting opposite Anya who looks about as serene as it's possible to look. If Anya wasn't so kind – she would really be getting on my nerves right now. Arggghhh. I just want it to be over.

TEXT! Wow, it could be Murphy. Why on earth would it be Murphy? He's totally disappointed in me for giving up on the breaks and going back to Killer Kennedy's rules.

Yep. Text is just Mum saying Good Luck. Thanks, Mum, but it's gonna take more than luck. I'm gonna have to dance the best I ever had.

1:00 p.m.

We're up. And breathe. I don't have a good feeling about this. I just don't think I can do it.

1:10 p.m.

I'm looking out from the side of the stage and I can see everyone. Mum looks about ready to burst with pride. Dad and Uncle Conor actually look to be talking to each other. That's pretty much a first. There's Aunty Stell who's looking round at what everyone's wearing, mainly disapprovingly. Siobhan and Ali look bored. Hey but not as bored as Eavanne and Sorcha who are behind them! Ha ha. I can't believe the school is so supportive of us all and have made everyone come to watch us – I mean, imagine if they made everyone go to a *Pulse* editorial meeting? Bor-ring. But wait, if the school has made everyone come along then that means that someone else must be here too. Come on, he *must* be here. Look! There's Dec and JP. He *must* be here. Why can't I see him? No, what am I thinking, Murphy would rather dress up as a big fluffy hamster and wander the corridors of the school rather than come to watch *this*. I bet he volunteered for litter picking or physics lab cleaning, anything rather than come to watch me.

At least I can count on my family, I suppose – oh look, there's Granny Nora getting out her special attention glasses. Hang on one minute, where does Rory think *he's* going? And why is he looking so suspicious? Oh this is just typical, there he goes fishing in his pockets for one of his mobiles. I can't believe he's leaving the auditorium just as I'm about to dance. Probably a 'big deal' he's got on that he's got to make a call about. Oh well, no chance to worry about that now.

They're calling my name. I'm on.

Weird, I feel weird. My legs are all saggy like the elastic in your pants when it's about to go, and I can't remember my moves, even though I know I know them inside out. I can't do this.

DANCE FROM THE HEART

1:30 p.m.
Well, I guess you could say I definitely danced from the heart!

I did it. And it was woop, woop, woop, woop, woop. I felt so free, so cool, so Aisling Louise Fitzsimons.

Rory had not left the auditorium to take a call from one of his friends. He'd actually sneaked into the sound booth. When I was on stage dancing, he started mixing one of his hip-hop tracks into the Irish Dance, so the two tracks were playing at the same time. The sound was different to any music anyone had heard before and I just knew both the Irish Dance and the hip-hop moves would work to the music. My heart felt it was beating right at the top of my throat and I could hardly breathe.

Suddenly it was just like it was that day at the beach,

I was just dancing for me and I didn't care about anyone else, I just couldn't help it. I danced my heart out and it felt so right. It felt so good, like that free bird.

When I had nearly got to the end I realized I had been dancing so hard I had my eyes closed. I did think about keeping them closed for another half an hour until everyone had gone home, but I couldn't hear anyone booing so I decided to chance it. I opened my eyes and lots of people were clapping along. Mum and Granny Nora were up on their tiptoes clapping madly. I think I saw Siobhan and Ali dancing as well. So I leaped up in the air and did my final Irish Dance Fusion move and with an Ali-style 'Da-dah' I was done. 'Ladies and Gentlemen, I give you Aisling Fitzsimons, the originator of competition-style Irish Dance Hip-Hop Fusion!'

And. Then. I. Saw. Murphy. He must have come in while I was dancing. He saw me dance! He saw me dance! He saw me dance!! Well I think he must have done, because he was high-fiving Dec and definitely looking in my direction. I felt so pleased he saw it. When you think about it, it's only because of him that I could even dance that way. I was trying to catch his eye, which is not easy when you're on stage in front of hundreds of people. I think I managed to give him a little nod of thanks, very difficult in an Irish Dance costume trying not to move.

Then I made the mistake of looking at the judges, who did not, I must say, look very happy. Then, suddenly, out of the darkness of backstage, I saw Killer Kennedy marching towards the judges on Full Flash Alert, like one of the ring wraiths from *Lord of the Rings*. Argghhh. I sure wasn't going to stay around to watch *that*, so before I knew it I was off the stage. I heard them announce my name to take a bow, but there was no way I was going back. I knew there was no way I was winning that competition. I'm pretty safe here backstage, and the four horses of the apocalypse (whatever they are) couldn't drag me back in front of the judges again. No way.

2:10 p.m.

I have a sneaky suspicion that my Irish Dance career might be well and truly over. Oh well, I'd better get my make-up off and take my hair down then. I can't start my new life with this amount of facial glitter on, can I?

From where I am backstage, I can hear the results coming through. I have my fingers crossed. For Anya, that is!! Why, what did you *think* I meant?

Oh no, here comes Siobhan. I'm sure she'll have something to say about 'my performance'. Well, whatever she says I hope she'll like the present I've got her – well, at the very least I can use it to defend myself against her Hard Stare.

2:15 p.m.

Siobhan said I was amazing. Her words. Ali too, he said what I did showed I had guts, because I did it *my* way. I guess it's true, I finally did what I wanted to do rather than what everyone else thought I should do. 'No,' Siobhan said, 'I meant being seen in that outfit.' Lol. They even want to work with me again on the Transition Project, which is sweet. Siobhan said, 'maybe, if we saw you in half two Aislings can cope with the workload' but I realized there's no need. If I'm not running around trying to please everyone then I should have plenty of time to do everything.

Siobhan was really touched by her backgammon set. Hopefully she'll be able to play with her Mum and Dad now. It would be great if she was involved with her family's hobbies like mine are. Well, my old hobby anyway.

Talking of families, Mum, Dad and Granny Nora were right behind Siobhan and Ali. Granny Nora could not stop smiling. I had to stop Rory from selling the rights to my performance to a big music label, he'd definitely got a little bit over-excited about the possibilities for Irish Dance Fusion. Dad looked really proud and Mum apologized loads for putting me under so much pressure. The thing is, I really don't think it was her fault. Her putting me under pressure only made me work harder at the Irish Dance and without knowing Irish Dance back to front there's no way I could've funked up the Irish Dance with Fusion. Without that and Murphy, anyway.

Two more people I needed to see before I awarded myself a queen-sized 'Aisling Goes Bananas' ice-cream sundae. First, Killer Kennedy. Gulp.

I didn't have to look far for Kennedy, she stopped me on the way out of the theatre. Amazingly, she said the judges were willing to overlook my 'little experiment' and she wanted me to come back to class on Monday. But I know deep down, Irish Dance is over for me. Thanks for asking, Mrs Kennedy, but no thanks. You won't be seeing any more of Aisling Fitzsimons in the Irish Dance classes. My dancing destiny lies elsewhere.

So that just leaves . . .

. . . Murphy.

3:35 p.m.

I didn't have to look far for Murphy – he was waiting for me in the corridor. He did, as usual, look off the scale of gorgeousness. But I played it cool, because after all, how hard is it to deal with just one Murphy when you've danced mad hip-hop fusion in front of an audience of hundreds? I was the coolest in this particular set-up, thank you very much. My play it cool attitude lasted all the way down the corridor. It lasted all the time it took to stand next to him and I was still working the cool stance right up until the time he came up really close to me, and looked me straight in the eye. Then it seemed to melt away, and I found myself rambling like a mad woman, again. This time though, I didn't care what I looked like or what he thought, I was just being me.

He said he wanted me to join his crew again, they're gearing up for another competition. Just because I've given up Irish Dance for the time being, it does not mean I'm taking up flashmobbing full time. Oh no. I'm still not over 'the library incident'. But, hey, that doesn't mean that nothing Murphy's got isn't of interest to me. If you know what I mean! In fact I'm really hoping that dancing isn't the only way we can spend some time together. After all, we *are* neighbours.

I did very kindly offer to show him a couple of my Aisling Fitzsimons patented moves: one a variation of one we did on the beach, and one new one which I've called 'On the Back of a Vespa' and it includes jumping piggyback on to Murphy's back and having him run me around. Not sure Kennedy would like that one, but *we* did, all the way down the corridor, all the way outside and all the way out of the school gates towards . . . well, towards . . . well, who knows what's next for me and Murphy. Oh and by the way, just in case you're interested, we kissed. For the first time and how was it? Oh I'd say every bit as good as dancing my heart out in front of a auditorium full of people.

Saturday 13 December
9:00–11:00 a.m.

At the gate for the flight. At least I *think* it's the gate, they haven't actually announced the gate number yet. Apparently although it says to be AT LEAST two hours before your flight, four hours is 'overkill'. Well, at least I'm gonna be on time for my flight. Because if I missed my flight I just don't think I could stand it. Like Dad said he couldn't stand me going on about being at the airport in plenty of time. Very funny, Dad.

Things have been loads better between us all since Dad's been made a director in Fitzsimons Plumbing. In fact everyone seems loads happier and Dad's director wages meant he could afford for me to go back to Boston for a week of the holidays. Hooray.

Somewhere over the Atlantic

I'm counting the minutes until I see everyone in Boston. I'm staying with Amelia, and Lauren and Colleen are all coming over on Monday and everyone's going to the ice-hockey game. It's gonna be a celebration. If I get my way it's going to be fajitas and Ben and Jerry's all round too.

I'm glad I told Amelia about me not really doing Irish Dancing any more. She said some of the older girls were trying out for the cheerleading team at Charlestown High and that she was thinking of doing that too. She said she was worried about telling me that, because she knows how much I was into Irish Dancing. Ha ha. To think I was really worried about telling her my news. Colleen sent me an email as well saying she was really looking forward to seeing me again. She said Phil and her were only ever friends as 'she'd never really felt right about it'. Well, I guess that's OK then. I don't mind, really. The whole Phil Donnelly episode seems like lifetimes ago. Hey maybe Phil and I could be friends too, that would be kind of cool. Because . . . well, because . . .

Murphy came round to see me just before we left for the airport, he brought me this cute little rabbit to take with me on my trip in a bag with loads of stars-and-stripes balloons and loads of my favourite candy bars (Star Bars) as he knows I can't get them in the States and he wanted Amelia and everyone to try them. I told you he was cute! He went all shy and said he thought I'd forget all about him in Boston. As if! Don't tell anyone but I've actually got a couple of pictures of Murphy to show Amelia, and I can't wait to show her all the footage of the flashmob. I was on Murphy's Bebo again – just to leave him a message – honestly, and I saw he'd changed his relationship status to 'seeing someone'. Know what Eavanne's says? 'Single.' Ha ha.

Rory has set up a whole website dedicated to the 'i-breaks and beats', as he calls the dance moves we invented. It's totally wild. He answers people's problems if they write in to him, and he's even got a blog. I swear I heard him on the phone to some Irish music label last night trying to 'secure sponsorship'. He's even talking to Murphy about getting his crew to donate some footage of their moves to show the main influences on i-breaks. But that's Rory.

It feels strange to think that I'm going home, I mean to Boston. I think about all the things that have happened to me in such a short time. Then I look out of the window over the Atlantic Ocean and I catch sight of my own reflection. I think I do look a *bit* different. Maybe I can see a little bit of Granny Nora in me.

How exciting not to know quite what's in store for me when I get back home to Dublin after my trip. Maybe Fitzsimons Plumbing will become the most successful plumbing business in Dublin. Hey, now we're all settled, maybe Mum will retrain as a plumber like Granny Nora. Rory could become the first internet millionaire in the

Fitzsimons clan. Maybe i-breaks and beats will catch on and I'll get the opportunity to open a chain of i-breaks schools like the David Beckham Academies.

But first, before any of that can happen, let there be ice cream, and lots of it.

Ais xx